A LETHAL JOKE

Also by Alice Zogg

Stand-Alone Mysteries

A Dark Book Club
A Bad Apple
Exposing the Past
No Curtain Call
The Ill-Fated Scientist
Accidental Eyewitness
A Bet Turned Deadly

R. A. Huber Mysteries

Evil at Shore Haven
Guilty or Not
Murder at the Cubbyhole
Revamp Camp
Final Stop Albuquerque
The Fall of Optimum House
The Lonesome Autocrat
Tracking Backward
Turn the Joker Around
Reaching Checkmate

A LETHAL JOKE

ALICE ZOGG

aventine press

This book is a work of fiction.

Published by Aventine Press
55 East Emerson St.
Chula Vista CA 91911
www.aventinepress.com

ISBN: 978-1-955162-25-8

Library of Congress Control Number: 2023911482
Library of Congress Cataloging-in-Publication Data
A LETHAL JOKE/ Alice Zogg
Printed in the United States of America
ALL RIGHTS RESERVED

To all my new friends at Westminster Gardens

CREDITS

Many thanks to Leo Schamadan for his help with my research relating to art, artists, and auctions pertinent to this book. Two decades ago, as I ventured into penning my first mystery novel, my daughter had volunteered to proofread the manuscript. Twenty years later, I am still taking advantage of her skills. Thank you, Franziska, for sticking with me through the years. Another fateful soul is fellow author Gayle Bartos-Pool, whose editing job is greatly appreciated. I value your talent, Gayle. This book was no exception when it came to the quiet and steady support of my husband, Wilfried. He showed the patience of a saint at times when I was glued to the computer and shut the world around me out.

CAST OF CHARACTERS

Norma Davenport The late Norma Davenport; was an eccentric

Derek Davenport Norma's son; has no time for games

Margo Davenport Derek's wife; likes to have peace and harmony

Elliot Davenport Norma's son; seems amused rather than alarmed

Paulette Davenport Elliot's wife; thinks that Norma's joke is in poor taste

Stella Osborn Norma's daughter; is often furious

Lucas Osborn Stella's husband; the silent type

Ava Vazquez Norma's daughter; is on her third marriage

Julius Vazquez Ava's current husband; is new to the family

Emma Ava's daughter; is away at college

Zabel Azarian Norma's companion; traveled with her late employer

Lilly	Zabel's friend; is currently on a trip to Australia
Bonita Robles	Norma's housekeeper; is a loyal employee
Sebastian Brunt	Art collector and auctioneer; is savvy in his field
Carla Brunt	Sebastian's wife; is a superb cook
Miles Rotterdam	Estate lawyer; carried out the late Norma's wishes
Earl Silverton	Financial advisor; tried to talk Norma out of her decision
Lieutenant Krop	Detective; is in charge of the murder investigation

CHAPTER 1

Norma Davenport died of natural causes on June 24 at her Laguna Beach, California residence, a week after her 81st birthday. The eccentric lady had opted not to have open heart surgery following her doctor's diagnosis of coronary artery disease. She was known to have said, "I've had a good life. If I die of a heart attack, so be it, but I refuse to be cut open."

On that fateful Saturday in June, cardiac arrest is exactly what struck her, two entire years after the doctor's verdict.

A widow during her last ten years, she had made the best of her situation by becoming an enthusiastic traveler. When that became difficult because of her health, she found other ways to amuse herself, and her traveling companion, Zabel, became her live-in companion. Toward the end of her life, her choice of entertainment was bizarre and held a bit of Schadenfreude.

Norma was survived by four children - - two sons and two daughters - - and five grandchildren. Her kids were past middle age, except for Ava, the youngest, who was still in her forties. Her offspring were scattered all over Southern California, out of state, and some of the grandkids even out of the country. They had their own busy lives to live and seldom made it to her neck of the woods. When they did, their relationship with their mother and grandmother was amiable.

This story is not about Norma's life, nor the circumstances of her death, but rather what transpired in the aftermath of her passing.

CHAPTER 2

On hearing of their mother's death, all four of her grown children flocked to the house that they had called home ever since Derek - - Norma and her husband's firstborn - - had been in the third grade. At that time, the Davenport children's father, a dentist, had furthered his education and had specialized in caps and implants dentistry, enabling them to live in a four-bedroom, two-story house close to the ocean at romantic Laguna Beach.

Even though it is officially a city, Laguna Beach, with its walkability and quaint charm, is regarded as more of a coastal village. When her husband died of cancer 10 years prior, Norma saw no reason to move. After all, the house was paid off in full.

With a little determination, the large residence could have accommodated the whole family, even though one bedroom was occupied by Norma's companion. The den had a sofa that pulled out into a bed. Regardless, Derek and his wife, Margo, chose to lodge at a nearby hotel. Elliot, Norma's other son, and his wife, Paulette, took over the master bedroom; daughter Stella occupied the guest bedroom with her husband, Lucas; and Ava with husband Julius made themselves comfortable in the fourth bedroom. The circular driveway came in handy, providing parking for all their cars.

Swollen-eyed and clearly distressed, Norma's companion, Zabel Azarian, asked Derek if she could stay on for a while until she could find another home. "Of course," he replied, "Stay as long as you want."

The siblings had a swift discussion of what needed to be done and then made arrangements. No great decision making was necessary, since their mother had it all prearranged and paid for. The funeral and interring of Norma's ashes was held on Wednesday, June 28. In addition to her four children and their spouses, only a handful of neighbors and friends, plus her companion and her housekeeper, Bonita Robles, attended. Many of Norma's friends had either passed away or were no longer able to make the journey to Laguna Beach.

Norma's grandkids lived in other states or abroad, and one, Ava's daughter, was still a sophomore at college in New York State. Grandma had told them in advance that there would be no reason for them to attend her funeral, as she did not believe young people should be exposed to such somber events. She hoped that they would remember her vibrant and alive. So, none made the trip.

CHAPTER 3

Having had a good cry during the funeral, Norma's sons and daughters became realistic the next day when they expected Miles Rotterdam, the estate lawyer, to read them their mother's last will and testament. The companion made herself scarce that day, to give them privacy.

On arrival, Mr. Rotterdam asked the family to gather in the den. When everyone was seated and facing the big screen, he said, "This is a bit unorthodox, but I am carrying out Mrs. Norma Davenport's wishes."

He then inserted a flash drive into the USB port of the smart TV, opened the video, and pressed "play."

To everyone's shock their mom appeared onscreen and she spoke these words:

"My dear children! When you view this video, I will have left this world. Don't be sad, I'm in good hands."

Some eyes got moist and Ava even cried audibly.

There was a pause and then the video recorder continued, *"Now to business. As you may remember, the stipulation in your father's and my wills was that if one of us dies, the other will inherit everything, and should we both die at the same time, our proceeds would be divided equally among our four children. Needless to say, at the time of your father's passing, I was the sole heir."*

Norma smirked before going on, *"It is my prerogative to use a bit of imagination when passing on my estate. My house here at Laguna Beach no longer carries a mortgage, and the proceeds from its sale will be divided equally among the four of you. It should go for about 3 million and change. If one of you chooses to live in it, I'm sure you will come to an agreement between siblings.*

As for the rest of my estate, that is 'finders keepers.' The deed to the house is in the safe. I hope all four of you will remember the portion of the safe's combination I entrusted each of you with."

The video concluded with Norma's image saying, *"Happy hunting! I love you all."*

There was total silence in the room as Miles Rotterdam extracted the flash drive from the TV. All the siblings and their spouses were stunned. To their inquiry of what else their mother left behind, Mr. Rotterdam replied, "That's all there is. I have a document in writing of the video content, which I'm leaving with you."

After the estate lawyer left, Derek was the first to speak, and he could not disguise his anger as he burst out, "What the hell does that mean, 'finders keepers'?"

Elliot grinned and stated, "Never a dull moment with our mom. She seems to amuse herself even beyond the grave."

Stella exclaimed, "Don't be morbid, Elliot!"

Then she addressed the rest and said, "Let's not jump to conclusions. Her investments paperwork is most likely in the safe and we'll each get a quarter of those funds. Let's go to the master bedroom where she keeps, or rather kept, the safe in her closet."

And she raised a finger for emphasis and added, "I sure hope we all know our parts of the combination."

CHAPTER 4

They had a hard time getting the safe open. The other three had no problem memorizing their part of the number combination, since it was the date of their respective birthdays, but Ava had difficulties. She had been given the task of recalling not only how many rotations between each number, but also in which direction the wheel had to be turned before getting to the numbers. At first, she could not remember the exact order, but after many unsuccessful attempts, they were finally able to turn the handle to access the safe.

They sighed with relief, unaware that their frustrations had only just begun.

Inside the safe there were two shelves. The deed to the house was on the top shelf, as were their mom's passport, birth certificate, and marriage license. No other documents could be found but there was a sealed envelope. Derek tore it open, and it contained a sheet of paper with a typed note, which read:

"My Tesla I bequeath to Zabel Azarian, my faithful companion. Her old Toyota has seen better days and I don't think any of my offspring are in dire need of a car."

The letter was signed, *"Norma Davenport"* and it was dated three months earlier. There was a PS: *"A copy of this statement is on file with attorney Miles Rotterdam."*

The bottom shelf contained a jewelry box, which was empty, except for one small compartment, holding a chain neckless with a ruby pendant, a diamond-and-ruby ring, and matching earrings. There was a folded note attached, and it read:

"I bequeath the ruby jewelry to my granddaughter, Emma, who always admired the set. As for the rest of my jewelry and valuables, like I said, it is finders keepers." The note was signed, *"Norma Davenport"* and also dated three months prior.

They were all at a loss for words and tried to come to terms with what they had found, or rather, what was missing.

Elliot recovered quickly and said, "Her important financial documents must be stored someplace else."

Ava's current husband, Julius, stated, "There is a file cabinet in the room we're using," and they all climbed the stairs to the bedrooms on the second floor.

They found some hanging folders in the file cabinet, containing banking and investment records of the past but nothing of the current nor the previous year. Many folders were empty with only names and phone numbers recorded inside, including the one for Miles Rotterdam and another for Earl Silverton.

Stella exclaimed, "Just our luck, Mom has gone paperless! We know Rotterdam but who is Earl Silverton?"

Derek said, "That's her tax guy and financial advisor. Remember, she told us a long time ago how wonderful he was."

"Well, we might be at his mercy, short of hacking into her computer. I don't see any folder with passwords. God only knows where she kept them."

"Maybe only in her crafty head," Elliot joked.

Ava said, "Good luck to you all with that. I, for one, am extremely hungry. The food that the housekeeper brought us when we first got here is long gone. I'm heading down to the kitchen in search of something edible for lunch."

There were eggs, some cheese, butter, and milk in the fridge but no bread. The freezer contained meats but nothing that could be fixed at a moment's notice. If I can find flour, I'll fix crepes, Ava told herself.

Lined up on the counter were three canisters. The first one she opened held rice; the next, sugar; and voila, the third contained flour. She found a mixing bowl in a cabinet and got to work.

She was about to place half a cup of flour into the bowl when the measuring cup hit something hard and round. She scooped up what looked like a round little ball, and to her amazement, the thing grew to a string of many little balls. She pulled the thing completely out of the canister and yelled, "What the heck!" while brushing the flour off the object.

Her husband, who had decided to see for himself what food there was to eat, was climbing down the stairs when he heard her outburst. He rushed to the kitchen, asking, "Everything okay?"

Ava turned to him, holding a strand of Mikimoto cultured pearls in her hand. She stammered, "I found this pearl necklace in the flour."

Before long, the rest of the family gathered in the kitchen, staring at Ava's find.

Elliot laughed out loud and then turned to Ava and said, "There you go: finders keepers." Then he addressed them all and continued, "I bet the rest of Mom's jewelry and who knows what else is hidden all over the house. Care to go on a scavenger hunt?"

"You're not funny," replied his brother.

Stella stamped her foot and said, "Elliot may be right. If so, that's infuriating."

Derek stated, "I'm in no mood for playing games and I'm sure the same goes for Margo."

His wife refrained from commenting. Paulette, the younger brother's spouse, spoke for the first time, saying, "I think we could all do with some food." And turning to Ava, she continued, "If you found something usable in the fridge, I'll help you fix it."

"Thanks for the offer," Ava replied, "there are enough ingredients to make cheese crepes. Everyone else, please get out of the kitchen."

Left to themselves, she continued adding the rest of the flour to the bowl, while she had Paulette beat four eggs lightly. Then they mixed the eggs and a little milk until a smooth mixture was obtained. Next, they added an entire cup of milk, one tablespoon of sugar, and a couple of knobs of butter.

Ava found a whisk with which she beat the mixture energetically. Then she greased a frying pan with a little butter, warmed it, and added some batter, distributing it evenly on the bottom of the pan, rotating it rapidly all around. She let the crepe brown for one minute on each side. Then Paulette filled it with cheese and rolled it up.

They made several more crepes and served them, one by one, as each was cooked. Soon, everyone's palate was satisfied but not their states of mind.

CHAPTER 5

Later in the day, and well into the night, the siblings found more gemstone jewelry throughout the house in odd places. Some of the locations were even practical for their mother when alive. As they combed through her wardrobe, they found gold and silver chain necklaces draped on hangers over several garments.

Ava commented, "That makes sense. This way she did not have to search through her jewelry box to find the perfect chain to go with her outfits."

The family members searched every room in the house and found more hidden treasures, but no documentation of any funds.

Zabel came back in the early evening and Derek asked her if she was aware of what their mom had been up to. She nodded and said that there was no harm in the little fun her employer had indulged in.

He then tried to press her for information about where they could find their mom's paperwork, or if she had access to the laptop computer in the den. Her answer was "no" to both, but she did mention that her employer went paperless two years earlier, around the time her doctor had made the diagnosis of coronary artery disease.

When he attempted to press her further, she excused herself by saying, "I'll give you folks some privacy," and promptly headed for the stairs and went up to her room.

Upon checking the garage, the siblings found a recent model blue Tesla parked next to an old Toyota. Storage shelves took up an entire wall, and they browsed through them, but no documents or a list of passwords came to light. They went as far as searching the attic, without any luck.

Since their mother had obviously gone paperless, they also rummaged through the house to hunt for flash drives, to no avail. Without a password, access to her computer was impossible.

They had pizza delivered for dinner and, late that night, they finally gave up the search. Derek and Margo drove to their nearby hotel while the rest went to bed.

CHAPTER 6

They had long turned off the lights but Derek and Margo lay awake.

Margo asked, "Can't sleep?"

"Obviously not," he shot back.

"Is it the hotel bed?"

"You know damn well it's not the bed," he replied. And without warning, the pent-up emotions he had suppressed all day came to the surface.

He blurted, "I really need the money and don't have time for mom's games. I told you about the losses I suffered in the stock market, but that's not all. I also showed poor judgement in other investments. I'm in a financial mess!"

Margo calmly said, "More things will show up at the house, maybe even some documents pertaining to Norma's finances. They may be in hiding places, just like the jewelry was. Think of the wonderful emerald and diamond ring you found among the pieces of her chess set. Surely that is worth several thousand dollars. How did you even think to look there?"

"I felt nostalgic. Mom and I used to play chess; she was an excellent player." And he changed the subject back to what was utmost on his mind, stating, "I need more than several thousand."

"Surely your part from the sale of the house will bring enough to cover your losses," she assured him.

"I can't wait. I need the money now."

"What if one of the others wants to live in it? That would help you out."

"I doubt that any of them would be in the position to buy me out in one lump sum."

After a long pause Margo asked, "What would you have done if your mother hadn't died right now, when you are in urgent need of funds?"

"I'd have had to apply for a loan and doubt that I could even get one with the way things stand. I'm facing bankruptcy."

Margo reached over and gently touched his hand, saying, "We'll find a solution. If all else fails, we can ask my parents for a loan."

"Thanks, but I don't want to do that."

Margo thought a change of subject might relax him and said, "Julius seems to treat Ava well. Do you think he has forgiven you for talking Ava into a prenuptial agreement?"

"I don't care either way. It had to be done, following her unsatisfactory experiences with men."

"I know her two marriages were unfortunate, but looking at it from Julius' point of view - -"

Derek interrupted, "You forget about the disaster with the fellow she was engaged to."

"Oh, I did forget about him. But I was going to say, Julius and Ava are both teachers and have approximately the same income, so you can't blame him to feel insulted."

"I've gone through this with Ava and didn't think I had to spell it out to you. It's not about the money Ava makes and not even about an eventual divorce. We all knew that Mom had little time left and now that she is gone, there is no dispute that Ava's portion of the inheritance is going to her, and only to her."

Margo smiled to herself. She had been able to divert his train of thought.

He switched the light back on, reached for a sleeping pill and the water glass on his nightstand at the ready.

Even though nothing was settled about his finances, the medication and his spouse had calmed Derek enough so that he was able to sleep. Margo, for her part, dozed off minutes later as she heard his regular breathing.

CHAPTER 7

At the Laguna Beach house people also had a hard time falling asleep. In the master bedroom, instead of closing her eyes, Paulette lay on her back staring at the dark ceiling and said, "Your mom's joke is in poor taste."

"You think so? I find it refreshing. She is having a bit of fun with us from beyond the grave. Good for her!" replied Elliot.

"I believe that her action provokes the worst in some of us."

"What do you mean?"

"Even though he is determined to hide it, I am positive that Derek is angry. And Stella is not even trying to hide her fury."

Elliot laughed out loud and stated, "They are bad sports. As for me, I'm having a ball. The necklace you found hanging inside the lampshade with the 'what are they called stones' - - -"

"Sapphire."

"- - - with the sapphire stones, sure made your eyes sparkle."

"True. I'm happy to have the necklace. But should we really do this 'finders keepers' stuff, or would it be better to divide the treasures we find equally, regardless of who finds them?"

"I don't care either way, but what Mom had in mind is more fun." And he asked, "Would you like to live in this house?"

After a pause she answered, "I haven't thought about it." Then she considered the idea and stated, "I'd love to! It's a wonderful home with a view to the ocean, plenty of shops and restaurants nearby, and only a ten-minute walk to the beach. Closest to paradise on earth you can get."

Then she sighed and stated, "But that's not going to happen. We couldn't buy the others out."

With that out of the way, they kissed good night and fell asleep instantly.

***

In the guest bedroom Stella pounded her pillow with her fists as she thought back to that day's events. Lucas, about to doze off, said, "Take it easy. Why are you so enraged?"

"How can you ask?" she shrieked.

"It's not like we're desperate for money."

"That's not the point. I can't tolerate being made a fool of."

"I see. You think that your mom was out to poke fun at you and your siblings."

"That's exactly what she's doing, even if she can't witness our humiliation."

"You've got that wrong. I knew her well enough to be certain that she loved you and your brothers and sister.

She amused herself by playing a little game with us all before her passing. What's the harm? In the end, you'll all inherit her estate, no matter the delay her diversion is causing. So be gracious and play along, the way she had intended it."

This was a long speech for a man of few words, and it surprised his spouse. But it did the trick, and they both fell asleep within seconds.

***

Across the hall, Ava and Julius did not seem to have a worry in the world. In fact, they were busy making love.

Later, satisfied and at ease, Ava stated, "I'm fortunate to have you. The losers I was married to before would have reacted differently to the situation we are in."

"How so?"

"They'd have aggravated my state of mind, instead of reassuring me, like you do."

"You never told me much about your previous marriages."

"There isn't anything to tell, other than the first was an irresponsible kid - - we were married straight out of high school - - and the next abused me on a regular basis."

"I'm glad I came to the rescue," Julius remarked with a smirk she failed to see in the dark.

Then he got serious and said, "Count your blessings. You will eventually get a fourth from the sale of this fabulous house, you'll get to keep whatever treasures you'll find, and you have the knowledge that your mother loved your daughter very much."

"True. She had a special relationship with Emma. How did you know?"

"She singled her out by specifically making her inherit the only jewels left in the safe."

That knowledge made Ava smile and she said, "I got a WhatsApp message from Emma today. She arrived safely in Florence, Italy, and will start on her exchange student program next week. I didn't have the heart to let her know about her grandma's passing yet, but will have to do it soon. A text won't do. I'll phone her in a day or two, as soon as she's settled.

On that sad note, they both dozed off.

***

Zabel Azarian lay awake too. She reflected on the past decade. Norma Davenport had been good to her. She not only mourned her as her employer but also as a friend. After losing her husband, the lady had put an ad in the paper, looking for a traveling companion to join her on an extensive European trip. The only requirement was that the person spoke some French. Armenia-born Zabel not only spoke French but was also fluent in several other languages, besides English. She answered the ad and got the job. And thus started a relationship that lasted ten years.

They took numerous trips together all over the globe, and Zabel, who had no living relatives in the US, eventually became Norma's live-in companion. Zabel was Norma's junior by 20 years, but their age difference did not matter; they got along great. When traveling became too much of a burden for Norma, they went to museums, concerts, plays, musicals, art exhibits, and other events together, or shared a simple stroll at the beach.

Zabel thought she may have been eccentric, but that's what made her and life in her house interesting. Funny how children take after their parents. She had seen pictures of Norma's late husband. Derek and Elliot had his brown eyes and bushy eyebrows, whereas the women had more delicate features like their mom's but didn't look alike. Stella was dark-haired, taking after her dad, and Ava was fair like Norma was.

A little lightheartedness gave way to her sadness when she thought of Elliot. He may have looked like his father, but he certainly had a bit of mischief in him, just like Norma. She wiped her eyes with the corner of the bedsheet and told herself, "Enough sentimentality, I need to find another home and decide what to do with the rest of my life."

The idea overwhelmed her and she fell into a restless sleep.

CHAPTER 8

Most of the siblings had jobs that allowed them to work away from their offices, which had been the norm ever since the pandemic. Margo had always worked from home as an editor with both well-known and midlist authors among her clients. Ava and Julius were teachers, off for the summer. Derek was CEO of a major company he could lead from afar.

As far as missing out on their exercise while away from home, most were not fanatical about it. Derek had exercise equipment at his home and some of the others had gym memberships in their respective towns, or played tennis and golf. But being away from those routines did not bother them much, at least not yet. The only obsessive exerciser among them was Ava, who was a jogger. She ran every morning at the crack of dawn, rain or shine.

It was only natural that Derek took charge. Early on Friday morning he had barely finished their continental breakfast at the hotel and had already made numerous business phone calls when he said, "I'm driving over to the house. They all need to know what's on the agenda for today. Are you coming with me?"

Margo replied, "I'm staying put. I've got to meet the deadline on two manuscripts. There are too many distractions over there and it's peaceful here."

Ten minutes later, Derek arrived at the house. He asked everyone to assemble in the den and announced, "We all need to stay in town until things are settled. You've brought your laptops and can work from here, so that shouldn't be a problem. A speedy settlement of the estate is important. Feel free to hunt for further hidden stuff, but I'm done with that. There are more pressing matters that need to be addressed."

He cleared his throat and continued, "I went over the documents of mom's will and living trust once more, which Miles Rotterdam left with us. I could not find any mention beyond what she told us in her video and the instructions she left in the safe. I went ahead and made an appointment with Earl Silverton, Mom's tax guy, for this afternoon. I sure hope that he can shed light on the matter. Any of you are welcome to come along. We also need to find an expert to evaluate the estate."

Elliot said, "Remember old Mr. Brunt?"

"Vaguely. I believe he had an art gallery in town."

"Correct. But besides the gallery, he also owned an auction house. I went to school with his son, Sebastian, who took over the business. I know this because we touched base at our high school reunion a few years ago. Paulette and his wife, Carla, also click. The four of us occasionally hang out together when we're in town. He showed us his impressive private art collection. Amassing master pieces seems to be an addiction with him."

"You don't have to tell me his life story," said Derek. "Just get in touch with the man and make him aware that this is urgent."

"Aye, aye, sir!" Elliot said and saluted.

"Are you mocking me? This is no time to clown around."

Elliot had a cynical reply on his tongue, but Paulette pressed her elbow into his and gave him a meaningful glance before he could utter it.

At that moment, the landline rang. Derek took the call which went like this:

Derek said, "Hello."

"Mr. Davenport?"

"Speaking."

"This is Bonita and I'm wondering - - -"

"Bonita?"

"Bonita Robles. Your mother's housekeeper. We met at the funeral."

"Oh yes, Mrs. Robles."

"I usually came to clean every other Monday and am wondering if you need me this coming Monday, July 3?"

Derek took a second to think it over and then said, "Thanks for the offer but we won't need your services in the next few days. Later, though, once the house is up for sale, we would appreciate a good cleaning. Please give me your phone number so that we can keep in touch."

Bonita gave it to him, and they ended the call.

He addressed the others again and inquired, "So who is coming along to see Earl Silverton?"

Stella said, "Lucas and I will," and turning to her husband, "Right, hon?"

Lucas nodded.

Elliot remarked, "I pass, since I have to work, and as far as I know, so does Paulette. I'm sure we can trust you with informing us of all the details you learn from the guy."

Ava nudged her husband and announced, "Count us out. After all, we're on summer break and I plan to make the best of it by showing Julius the sites of my hometown." And with a grin she added, "I'm certain that you and Stella can handle the interview with the financial advisor on your own."

Zabel stuck her head in the door and said, "Just want to let you folks know that I'm off to go home hunting," and left.

Derek stated, "That's all for now," then followed his mom's companion to the attached garage. He caught up with her as she was about to step into the Tesla's driver seat.

He said, "Just making sure you know how to handle this beauty."

"Don't worry. Norma had me drive it often when she didn't feel up to the task," Zabel replied.

"Good. As you know, Mom was full of surprises. I'm sorry that she has left you nothing in her will besides the car."

"Oh, there was no need. She was plenty generous to me when alive."

That stated, Zabel got in the car, pressed the garage opener, and drove away.

Derek's siblings and in-laws were still gathered in the den when he got back, bursting out, "That woman knows something, I'm sure of it!"

CHAPTER 9

It only took Derek 20 minutes to drive them to Earl Silverton's office in Irvine and they arrived at the appointment on the dot.

While riding the elevator up to the top floor of the ten-story building, Stella asked, "As Mom's financial advisor, the man must be in possession of all her investment documents, correct?"

Derek said, "I should hope so," and Lucas just squeezed her arm in a calming gesture.

The receptionist, or possibly his business partner, ushered them into Mr. Silverton's domain. He got up from behind his desk to greet them, then motioned them into seats facing him and sat back down.

Stella couldn't help herself and, looking out the large windows taking up an entire wall, exclaimed, "What a spectacular view!"

Derek was not in the mood to admire any view. He came straight to the point and addressed Earl Silverton, saying, "Like I informed you over the phone, we are here to inquire into our mom's finances. She apparently went paperless, so we are seeking information from you."

Silverton nodded, then looked in Stella's direction and said, "As I've already expressed to your brother, I am sorry for your loss."

Then he got down to business and addressed Derek, stating, "After your call I familiarized myself with your mother's records, dating back two years." And glancing at each one in turn, he asked, "What exactly do you want to know?"

Derek took charge again and stated, "Mom's estate lawyer informed us of her will. She left us her house, but for the rest, it is 'finders keepers,' as she put it." And he explained the bizarre treasure hunt that took place.

Silverton chuckled and said, "Your mother was an unusual lady and quite unconventional, but I would humor her if I was in your shoes. Indulge her in the joke, what's it going to hurt?"

After a pause he got serious and inquired, "Again, what can I help you with?"

Stella blurted, "We can't find any documents or information about her investments nor her savings."

"That's because there aren't any to speak of, as far as I know." Silverton replied.

All three stared at him. After the initial shock Derek said, "Come now! We happen to know that Dad left her with substantial money when he died and that you managed her finances ever since. So, what's up?"

"True, I invested her money - - wisely - - if I may say so, until about two years ago. Then she came to see me one day and demanded that I liquidate it all and give her the cash. In some of the transactions there were penalties to pay for early withdrawal, but she did not care. I tried to talk her out of the decision and pointed out that keeping her funds invested was in her best interest and of course would make her more money. She insisted that the monthly annuity disbursements and her social security income was all she needed to live on, and that she wasn't interested in amassing more money."

He sighed and added, "Like I said, I tried to dissuade her but to no avail. Her mind was made up."

"What the heck did she do with her money, spend it all?" Derek roared. "According to my calculations, Dad left her with more than half a million. Over the last ten years, if invested wisely, that amount should have increased."

Earl Silverton calmly answered, "On that day two years ago, she wrote a check in the amount of $100,000 to her companion, and another in the amount of $50,000 to her housekeeper. What she did with the rest, I have no idea. She no longer required my services as financial advisor from that day onward."

They could not get more information out of the man, but it was not for the lack of trying. He either did not know what happened to the rest of the funds or was sworn to silence.

On the ride back to Laguna Beach Stella asked, "So what do we do now?"

"Beats me," her brother replied. "For all we know the three to four-hundred-thousand cash is buried in Mom's backyard."

CHAPTER 10

Meanwhile, at the late Norma Davenport's residence, Elliot and Paulette took a break from their laptops and sat at the kitchen counter, enjoying a cup of coffee.

Paulette remarked, "Ava's new husband is nice, don't you think?"

"Sure. Let's hope he stays that way. Ava has a knack for marrying losers."

Their conversation then turned to what was utmost on their minds. Paulette said, "I've been thinking about what you asked me the other night. In fact, the idea of us living in this house won't leave me alone. I hope that it's possible. Maybe Derek and Stella will come back from the financial advisor guy with good news."

"I'm counting on it," Elliot replied. "Mom must have left us enough capital to buy the others out. She did a lot of traveling for a while but couldn't possibly have gone through all the money Dad left her. I'm glad you're warming up to the idea of living here. That's what I had in mind myself all along. Work is no problem; we can do our jobs from anywhere. I still have some friends in this neck of the woods, and there is plenty of fun stuff to do in this sleepy little hometown of mine."

With that happy plan in mind, they both went back to work. Elliot had his office setup in the den, and Paulette went upstairs to her laptop in the master bedroom.

***

Zabel stepped into her newly inherited Tesla on that Friday, June 30, parked on a side street off the condominium she had just viewed. She sat motionless for minutes, exhausted. It was close to evening, and she was done for the day looking for a new home. She had been to several open houses in Orange County - - Irvine, Huntington Beach, Seal Beach - - and finally ended up at the city of Long Beach in L. A. County.

Nothing was what she considered "doable." She either did not like the place, or it was beyond her price range. Sure, the money from Norma, which she had carefully invested, was more than enough for a down payment, but she needed to be able to pay the mortgage on a monthly basis. Maybe looking for a job first would be a better plan, she decided. But what could she do? Teach art classes at a junior college? As Norma's companion, she had been out of the job market for ten years. It won't be easy, she mused.

Then she dwelled on the immediate problem at hand. She asked herself, do I need to tell the family what I know? Norma's children and their spouses seem like nice people, but she told me to keep the secret for a while, giving them time to figure it out for themselves. I'll sleep on it, she decided. Right now, I need to find a place to have a bite to eat. She searched her GPS for restaurants nearby and then drove off.

After arriving home in Laguna Beach that night, she thought, I don't need to limit myself to the coast. It may be too hard to find a job in a beach town. With that in mind, she called her old friend, Lilly, who taught at Pasadena City College. Lilly was sympathetic to Zabel's dilemma and invited her to spend the weekend at her home in Arcadia, so that they could discuss her friend's options in detail. Zabel was more than happy to accept, since she was uncomfortable living in the same house among Norma's heirs under the circumstances.

***

The Vazquezes had walked around the downtown village of Laguna. Like a tour guide, Ava had taken Julius to St. Francis by the Sea, one of the smallest cathedrals in the world. The Church had plenty of old-world charm with its wooden bell tower, antique chandeliers, Spanish tiles, and stained-glass windowpanes.

Then they had strolled along Pacific Coast Highway, browsing many blocks of shops, from high-end boutiques to art galleries and everything in between. They spent time inside the Laguna Art Museum and ended up at Heisler Park, set on the bluff. Julius was impressed with the spectacular views to the ocean, the tide pools, and the neatness everywhere, including the restrooms. They sat on a bench and watched the surfers, at peace with the world, it seemed.

It was not until the end of their outing when they dined on salmon at a seafood restaurant that Ava brought up the subject both had avoided all day, but had not been able to shake from their minds.

She said, "I'm counting on Derek and Stella bringing back good news from the financial advisor."

Julius asked, "How much money is at stake?"

"About half a million, I guess."

There was a sudden flicker of greed in his eyes as he stated, "A fourth of that is not too shabby."

To say that all four siblings and their spouses went to bed disappointed on that Friday night would be a gross understatement.

CHAPTER 11

On Saturday morning Sebastian Brunt stopped by.

Elliot greeted him at the door and said, "Thanks for coming on such short notice."

"Anything for an old friend," the art collector replied. And he added, "Welcome back to my neighborhood. As you know, I live in my folk's old house since they passed."

Elliot introduced him to the rest of the family, who gathered in the kitchen and dining room, fixing or finishing their breakfasts. Ava was still in her running shorts.

Sebastian remarked, "I saw you jogging by my house a while ago."

"I run every morning," she replied.

Derek, who had arrived early at the house and was full of nervous energy, had enough of the chit-chat and took charge.

He said, "We'd greatly appreciate your appraisal of our mom's belongings and a speedy liquidation. Last night, I had all my siblings and my wife choose what they want to keep for themselves and label the items with a blue masking tape sticker. Some will take the good dishes, others special mementos. The rest is up for sale."

And he stressed, "The beds and other essential furniture will have to stay until we are ready to leave but everything else needs to be settled as soon as possible."

Elliot said, "It's obvious that my brother is in a big hurry."

Derek dashed him an angry glance but did not comment.

Sebastian turned to him and said, "I can see that you are organized." And with that, the three of them toured the house.

The art collector took his time, looking at objects and studying each. He said little, but kept notes. They started upstairs, going into every bedroom, then all the rooms on the ground floor, ending up in the living room.

At the end of his scrutiny, Sebastian chose to sit on an upholstered chair facing the brothers, who plopped themselves down on the sofa.

He looked at his notes and then said, "Your mom had a good eye. There are things of value in this house. There is a Tiffany lamp in the master bedroom, a nice collection of Lladro figurines in the guest bedroom, and bronze sculptures crafted by well-known artists throughout the house. In the dining room I noticed several silver sets exhibited on the display cabinet."

He looked up from his notes and stated, "As to furniture, there are a few valuable antiques. The secretary in the den and that cabinet with the silver in the dining room are exquisite. And so are these," he pointed at the two end-tables flanking the sofa.

He glanced around the room with professional curiosity and said, "I noticed a blue sticker on the polished ebony upright piano. Who plays?"

Derek replied, "Stella, our sister, and my wife both do." And embarrassed he admitted, "There is a bit of a dispute of who'll get it, but we'll figure it out."

"Well, whoever ends up the winner should take good care of it. It is desirable as far as pianos go."

"What about the paintings?" Derek asked, eager to change the subject.

"I was getting to that. There are numerous works of art hanging on walls throughout the house. The paintings of the well-known artists are not originals - - they are prints or good reproductions.

He added with a smirk, "If they were the real thing, I wouldn't mind having one or two in my own private art collection."

Elliot put in, "There are some originals among the bunch. Right?"

"Absolutely, but they are creations by painters I am unfamiliar with. Some are good but are most likely the works of unknown artists. I will have to do research on those."

Sebastian got up and examined a pair of pastels in ornate frames that hung on the wall above the two end-tables once more. They were both ocean scenes with a sandy beach in the foreground; one having a sailboat in the distance, the other a couple of surfers. The signature at the bottom of the right-hand corner was a simple Z. A.

The auctioneer stated, "These two works are excellent samples of its kind but of little value since the artist is unknown. But the frames by themselves should fetch a substantial amount." And chuckling he said, "This Z. A. must not have a big ego, or he or she would have at least acknowledged part of the name." As an afterthought he remarked, "I imagine that the person is either a local artist or was a personal friend of your mother's."

"Why do you think so?" Elliot wanted to know.

"There are three more works by Z. A. in the house; two in the companion's bedroom, and one in the guest bedroom."

"I agree. It makes sense that Mom knew the artist."

Sebastian sat back down and said, "All in all, there are many interesting pieces of value at this residence."

"Amounting to six figures?" Derek asked.

Sebastian laughed and Elliot rolled his eyes.

"I'm serious."

Sebastian turned somber and said, "Sorry. I thought you were joking. I would say in the $50,000 range at best, including the furniture. Unless one of the famous paintings would be authenticated as the real thing, which is almost impossible in my opinion."

He sensed Derek's disappointment and quickly said, "One never knows with auctions, though. If a person is gung-ho on a certain object, the bidding can go up drastically, way beyond the piece's worth."

"How soon can you auction the things off and what's your cut in it?" asked Derek.

"I can have my employees make a truck pickup this afternoon. Once in our possession, everything needs to be inventoried, labeled, and listed. I also need to have time to advertise the items in our weekly brochure. The Fourth of July is coming up on Tuesday, so that will delay the process. The earliest I can do the auction is a week from today, Saturday, July 8, and that's putting a rush on it. And as far as our fee, we usually take 20% of the sale price, but since Elliot is a friend, I'll make it 15%."

Before his brother had a chance to say anything more, Elliot stated, "That's great! Thank you for giving a rush order and thanks for the discount. We really appreciate it."

Sebastian addressed his friend, "Are you planning to stay in town for a while? Carla and I would like to invite you to dinner at our house. She's going to be in an amateur theater production and is busy with rehearsals right now, but in a couple of weeks that will be over."

"Sounds wonderful. Thanks! We must stay put until Mom's estate is settled, so are looking forward to it." He turned to his brother and explained, "Carla is Italian and fixes the most delicious gourmet meals. Her veal piccata is superb!"

Derek tried to be polite despite having heard enough of pleasantries and said, "You're a lucky man, Mr. Brunt."

About to leave, Sebastian handed them a contract to sign and later that afternoon, his employee gave them a receipt listing all items that were being hauled away.

CHAPTER 12

The Osborns were spending Sunday afternoon at the beach. Stella sat in her beach chair under their sun umbrella. She looked up from the mystery novel she was reading and watched Lucas getting out of the water and then walking toward her, careful not to splash sand on folks sprawled on their towels.

She thought, he may be past fifty but still looks good in his bathing trunks. And she mused further, I don't look too shabby myself, even though I no longer dare to wear bikinis.

As he toweled himself off, she asked, "How's the water?"

"Refreshing," he replied.

"That's what I like about you, always the optimist. Most people would have said 'cold.'"

He shrugged and thought, the Pacific is always cold at the beginning of summer, but did not comment. Lucas was the silent type. Any unnecessary conversation he considered worthless chatter.

As Lucas got comfortable next to her, she buried her head back in the book but could no longer concentrate. There was too much on her mind.

She burst out, "The nerve of Derek! Telling us we have the day off from what he calls 'getting Mom's estate in order.' I can't believe he even said, 'Feel free to attend Church or explore the town.' What makes him think he can tell us what we can and can't do?"

As her voice rose, they got annoyed glances from their beach neighbors.

Lucas reached over and touched her shoulder lightly, which calmed her. She had not expected an answer from her spouse and continued in a lower voice, "He assumes we're happy that he put himself in charge but seems to forget that we're all capable adults. Yesterday, before Sebastian Brunt's people came to take everything away for the auction, he told me to empty out the secretary and carefully arrange its content in the built-in linen closet. Like I'm incapable of making any decision on my own!"

Lucas put an end to that conversation by saying, "Taking charge comes naturally to Derek; he's a CEO. You should be relieved he has taken the responsibility."

Soon he lay on his back with eyes closed and hands folded behind his neck and stated, "This is paradise."

"True," Stella agreed. "I only realize now how lucky our family was to grow up here."

For the next few minutes, flashbacks from her childhood popped into her mind. Picnics on this very beach, where they played with frisbees and badminton off season and enjoyed swimming and water games in the summer. And looking back, she realized what a happy couple her parents were, holding hands more often than not.

She suddenly asked, "Would you like us to move to Laguna Beach and take over Mom's house?"

"We can't afford to buy the others out."

"We could, if we found the missing cash."

"So far there is no trace of that extra cash and it may never surface. Don't make any plans and don't get your hopes up."

CHAPTER 13

On Monday, July 3, Zabel was driving back from her friend Lilly's home in Arcadia. Traffic was heavy. People must get ready for Independence Day, she thought. The normally one-hour-and fifteen-minute drive was taking close to two hours, plenty of time to reminisce about what decisions her friend had helped her make.

Her mind was made up: She was going to relocate to Pasadena or nearby, where there were better job opportunities for her. She had also confided in Lilly about the dilemma she found herself in, concerning the Davenport family. Her friend had advised that, regardless of the promise she'd made Norma, now was the time to tell her heirs what she knew. Zabel decided that she would go ahead and enlighten them, first chance she got.

Then she thought, Lilly must be on her way to the airport by now. Even though her friend had been busy packing and getting ready for her trip to Australia, she had taken the time to discuss and advise Zabel on making decisions for the future. What a great pal! Zabel had offered to drive Lilly to the airport, but her friend had said, "Don't be silly, that's too much out of your way. I've already arranged for an Uber."

Zabel was starting to look forward to relocating to the San Gabriel region and to a new chapter of her life. She was a realist, however, and knew that job opportunities for her at age 60 were limited. Still, Lilly had convinced her that, as a talented artist and being fluent in several languages, she was by no means out of the work market.

By the time she neared Laguna Beach, it was noon. Although she had had breakfast with her friend just before leaving town and was not hungry for lunch, she longed for a cup of tea when reaching the house she still considered "home" at that point.

Zabel would not get the chance to either drink tea nor have that talk with the family.

CHAPTER 14

At the house they were working in teams to get it "decluttered," using Derek's term. The men were tackling the attic and the garage, Margo and Paulette sorted out clothing and linens, while Stella and Ava sat in the den, rifling through numerous photo albums.

Their brothers were leaving it up to them to decide which albums would be kept by which sibling. It turned out that those decisions were harder to make than expected, since many of the photos were of interest to them all. The sisters took their task seriously and put a lot of thought into their choices.

They became nostalgic when inspecting pictures from decades ago, when they were kids. Stella said, "Look at this one! That was taken at the Champs-Élysées in Paris on our family trip to Europe. Dad and Mom sure were a handsome pair."

"And had cute kids," Ava added with a giggle.

A couple of albums later, she exclaimed, "Oh! That was my sweet sixteen party. You were already at college at the time."

Their journey into the past continued. No wonder they hardly made a dent in organizing the photos and putting them in chronological order.

In the master bedroom, standing inside the walk-in wardrobe closet, Margo said to Paulette, "Our mother-in-law sure knew how to dress. Everything is chic, whether designer labeled or not."

Paulette nodded, then held up a blouse and exclaimed, "Look at this! Isn't it darling? Too bad it doesn't fit me or I'd keep it for myself."

They were taking the garments over to the queen-size bed, folding each carefully, and storing them in plastic bags, separating slacks, capri pants, shorts, tops, ensembles, and dresses. The wardrobe closet contained summer clothes and a few lightweight cardigans. They would get to the winter clothes and coats in the fourth bedroom later.

Several bags were already full and they had not even made a dent in the items still on hangers when Paulette remarked, "It's a shame that all this is going to the Goodwill. Too bad Norma wore a petite size. I can't think of anyone I know that would fit into her clothes."

Margo thought about it and then stated, "Most are size 6 or 8 petite. I bet the housekeeper - - what was her name again? - - could fit into some."

"Good idea. Mrs. Robles is little. We'll ask if she wants some of the outfits."

That settled, they broke for lunch.

They had food delivered from a Mexican restaurant nearby and all eight ate at the long table in the dining room.

Swallowing the last bite, Elliot said, "I can't believe the stuff that's gathering dust in the attic. There is luggage of all shape and sizes; an enormous number of boxes with not only Christmas, but numerous year-round holiday decorations; two sets of golf clubs; skis and boots; and a bunch of things that probably haven't been used in decades."

Ava laughed and said, "The last time Mom skied that I know of was twenty years ago. What about golf, was she still playing before she got diagnosed with heart disease?"

At that very moment the door to the attached garage opened as Zabel let herself in. She stuck her head in the dining room door and said, "Hello, I'm back. *Bon appetite!*" Then she glanced around and asked, "What happened to the rest of the furniture?"

Derek replied, "They took everything that we don't absolutely need away to be auctioned off next Saturday."

"I see," she said and was about to go up to her room but decided to peek into the living room first.

Derek turned back to his sister and said, "To answer your question about Mom's golf - - -"

There was a loud outburst in the next room and everyone hurried over. Zabel pointed to where the pastels had hung and stammered, "They're gone, my paintings are gone!"

"Your paintings? You mean Mom gave them to you?"

Zabel did not answer but asked instead, "Where are they?"

"I assume at the auction house."

"The Brunts'?"

"Yeah. We'll call them."

"Never mind," Zabel said. "I know the location." And she was out the door.

CHAPTER 15

The siblings and their spouses were tongue-tied for a moment, stunned by Zabel's outburst and rushed exit.

Stella suddenly cried out, "Of course! She's the artist."

"What are you talking about?" asked Derek.

"Her last name is Azarian. The Z. A. signature on the paintings stand for Zabel Azarian. How could we have been so blind?"

Margo put in, "No wonder we found additional works of hers in the rest of the house. I can understand that she's upset. We got rid of her babies while she was gone."

Derek said, "I'm sure she's getting her paintings back. The auction is not until Saturday. She should have told us that those pastels are her work. I barely glanced at the two letters she apparently used instead of a signature, which is odd. And that's not the only thing she's leaving us in the dark about. I bet that woman knows what Mom did with the missing funds."

***

The person parked at the curb on a side street, then kept an eye out on the few parking spaces behind the

Brunt auction house. There were only three cars parked in the small lot, and one was the blue Tesla. After waiting five minutes but what felt like hours, the individual had second thoughts. What if the suspicion was wrong and Zabel knew nothing about the missing money? Suddenly feeling silly, the person had a change of mind and was about to drive away when the back door to the auction house opened.

Zabel stepped out, followed by Sebastian and his employee, carrying all five of her paintings and loading them into the Tesla. The auctioneer waved to her as she drove out of the mini lot.

The person watching dropped the newspaper that had worked as a screen, put the engine into gear, and also drove off.

***

Four hours later, there was a ring at the Davenport's front door. Norma's daughters were still sorting through photo albums and the rest were busy elsewhere in the house. At the second ring, Stella finally went to answer it and found a Laguna Beach police officer at the entrance.

He said, "Is this the residence of Zabel Azarian?"

"For the moment, yes."

The officer was clearly uncomfortable as he said, "I'm afraid I have bad news. There has been an accident on Pacific Coast Highway. I am sorry to inform you that Ms. Zabel Azarian did not survive the crash."

CHAPTER 16

Even though the Davenport clan had had no specific plans for the Fourth of July, Zabel's fatal accident put a damper on the holiday. The official news by that morning was that Zabel had either fallen asleep at the wheel or had suffered a medical emergency as a result of her car crashing full speed into a building when going around a curve on Pacific Coast Highway. Although there was substantial damage to that structure, nobody inside the building was hurt. An autopsy on Zabel's body was pending.

Derek had them all gathered in the den again, since they needed to make decisions once more.

Julius said, "She did look tired yesterday when we saw her for a brief moment."

"Nonsense," said Elliot. "The way she dashed out of here didn't look like she was tired at all."

Derek said, "Let's not speculate. The authorities will let us know what happened once they're done with their analysis." And he took charge like always and stated, "As far as we know, Zabel has no living relatives in the US. We must go through her personal items to search for an address book. We need to try to notify her friends."

"What about funeral arrangements?" Ava asked.

"That was next on my agenda to discuss. Chances are slim that we'll find a will with possible instructions in her belongings, so that unpleasant task is up to us. The unfortunate circumstance we find ourselves in delays getting the house ready for sale. I suggest we all chip in for an inexpensive interment and get things settled as soon as her body is released."

Stella shouted, "All you care about is a speedy settlement of Mom's estate. Never mind that her faithful companion died only yesterday. We owe her a beautiful funeral with all the bells and whistles."

"I doubt that the lady cares, one way or the other from where she is now. Funerals are for the people left behind, and she does not seem to have any."

"You don't have to be so crude!"

Margo, forever the peacemaker, stated, "Both of your points of view have merit. For now, let's search Zabel's room for any kind of useful information."

And Elliot, forever the joker, turned to Ava and said, "Well, Sis, since our stay here seems to be prolonged indefinitely, I may have to join you on your daily runs."

"I doubt that you'd be able to keep up," she teased back.

On the next day, the authorities informed the family of two things: Number one, the Tesla was beyond repair; in other words, totaled. Number two, the autopsy of Zabel's body revealed a large amount of sedative drugs in her stomach. In other words, she lost consciousness due to an overdose of sleeping pills, and the car kept going and crashed itself into the building.

The case now went from an accidental death to a full-blown murder investigation. As for Norma's descendants, they were in denial that their mother's joke could have had a lethal consequence.

CHAPTER 17

Lieutenant Krop of the Laguna Beach City Police Department was the detective in charge of the Zabel Azarian case. Homicides were not the norm in his jurisdiction, but on the rare occasions when there was murder, he handled the investigations not only with shrewdness but also with tact.

On that first day of inquiry, July 5, he spoke to the Davenport heirs as a group, getting the basic data on Zabel Azarian. He learned that she had been born and raised in Armenia, became widowed early in life, never remarried, and had no children. In fact, she had no relatives in the USA they knew of. For the last ten years, Zabel Azarian became their mother's trusted live-in companion.

Lieutenant Krop said, "That's all clear. Now let's get to the gist of the matter. When was the last time you saw Ms. Azarian?"

As usual, Derek decided to be the spokesperson of the group. He stated, "She had been visiting a friend over the weekend and came back - - -"

The detective interrupted, "What is the friend's name and where does he or she live?"

"I think she mentioned someone named Lilly but gave no last name." He glanced at the others and asked, "Does anyone know where Lilly lives?"

Paulette said, "I think Zabel said Pasadena, or it might have been Altadena."

Addressing Derek again, the detective said, "Please continue."

"We were all eating lunch when she came back on Monday. She said hello to us in the dining room, but then made a discovery in the living room and rushed off again, not even bothering to take her luggage up to her room first. We assume that she went to an auction house in town but of course can't be sure."

"Which auction house?"

Derek replied, "The Brunts'. Sebastian Brunt and my brother are friends."

"Explain why you think she went there."

Derek informed the detective that her artwork had been taken from the property to be auctioned off because the family had not known that Zabel was the artist. That explained the five paintings that were found in the trunk of the Tesla, Lieutenant Krop thought. Amazing that there was hardly any damage to them, considering that the car was totaled. He did not share any of this with the people of interest in the suspicious death of Zabel Azarian. He was here to get information from them, not the other way around.

Instead, he asked, "How much luggage, and where is it now?"

"Just an overnight bag. We took it up to her room."

The lieutenant stated, "I'm going to have a look at it before I leave. Right now, I'm interested in your movements on Monday, July 3."

It was established that they had spent the morning sorting through their late mother's things. When Zabel stormed off, they had just finished eating lunch and took a break from the tedious task of going through the deceased's possessions. Then they continued with their work until 6:30 in the evening, when some went out to eat and others stayed put.

Their alibis were impossible to validate, since they all vouched for each other. The lieutenant took it all with a grain of salt but was confident that in the end he would be able to determine if they were all telling the truth.

He ordered, "I hope none of you were planning to leave Laguna Beach anytime soon. I will have to take down your statements individually within the next few days."

Before leaving, he went up to Zabel's room in search of clues. He found nothing of interest in her carry-on luggage. There was a ledger in the top drawer of her desk, listing Lilly under "L" with no last name or address, only a telephone number. He stored that number into his phone. The rest of the address book contained names and numbers of places like hair salon, auto mechanic, manicure/pedicure, and doctors.

The lieutenant remembered that the phone they had found on the victim's person had also only a few numbers listed in her contacts. The woman either had memorized lots of numbers by heart or led a secluded life.

As soon as the detective was out the door, Margo said, "Do you think he considers us as suspects?"

"Could be," said Elliot.

"We hardly knew her. How could we have a motive to kill her?"

"Don't act dumb! Like Derek pointed out more than once, Zabel knew where Mom's extra money is stashed away. Dragging that information out of her and then having the loot all to oneself is motive enough."

Derek stated, "But the lieutenant won't know about the missing money, unless one of you blabs to him." And there was raw emotion in his voice as he stressed, "No matter what the man thinks, the culprit is not one of us. Mom didn't raise a killer."

Stella, who had not fully listened to their conversation since her mind was stuck on something else, blurted, "So we can't even leave town! I sure hope the lieutenant is wrapping things up soon. Lucas and I are booked on a river cruise in Europe at the end of the month."

"We all have plans for this summer, sis, you're not the only one," Elliot shot back.

CHAPTER 18

They were in a wild rush at the auction house to get everything ready for the auction in only three days. Sebastian was all over the place, directing traffic, so to speak. The labeled and listed items were being moved to a room for advanced viewing, taking place on Friday, the day before the auction. Everything else still needed to go through the process.

He was hollering at an employee, "No, no! Not the large bronze, it hasn't been tagged yet. Bring it back," when the detective entered the place.

He showed his credentials and, trying to make himself heard above the noise of workers, shouted, "I'm Lieutenant Krop. I'd like to have a word with you. Can we talk someplace quiet?"

"This is not a good time, but I can give you a few minutes. Follow me," Sebastian said, and led the way to a small sitting room adjacent to the auction hall.

Once there, he didn't offer him a chair and said, "So what's this about? I'm extremely busy right now."

The lieutenant said, "I'll be brief. I understand that Ms. Azarian came to see you this past Monday."

"Who?"

"Zabel Azarian."

"Oh, Zabel! Yes, she did. There was a mishap about her artwork but I gave it back. So why are you here?"

"She drove her car into a building on Pacific Coast Highway Monday afternoon, March 3, and was killed."

"So that was her! I heard it on the news but no name was mentioned. That's a nasty curve her car spun out. What a tragic accident."

"It was no accident. I'm looking into her homicide and you may have been the last person to see her alive."

Sebastian stared. Seconds later he said, "Hold on! How can it be homicide if she drove her car into a building?"

"She was drugged." And the lieutenant continued, "Tell me all about the business you had with Zabel Azarian."

Sebastian pointed to a lounge chair and, sitting down on another, said, "This seems to take longer than I thought. She came to me in a fury demanding her pastels back. You see, they were picked up by accident with all other items the Davenport family is having auctioned off on Saturday. They didn't know it was Zabel's art and neither did I. I gave all five paintings back to her, minus two frames, and had her sign a receipt for them."

He went to a credenza, found the receipt book in its top drawer, and pointed out the appropriate page.

The detective glanced at it and nodded. Then he asked, "What did you mean with 'minus two frames'?"

"The frames of the two pastels that hung in the Davenports' living room are valuable. I decided to sell them separately since the artwork itself is from an unknown artist. I told Zabel that if she could wait, I'd put the pictures back into the frames. She didn't want them, explaining that the late Mrs. Davenport had purchased the frames and that their proceeds should go to her heirs."

"At what time did Ms. Azarian come to your auction house?"

"I didn't check the time but it was shortly after lunch; I'd say about 12:20 or 12:30 at the latest."

"How long did she stay?"

"Not long. I went in search of her five pastels, and then my employee and I helped her load them into her trunk. She was only here about ten minutes or so. You can't honestly think I had anything to do with her death?"

The lieutenant said, "I have to cover all angles."

"At what time was the crash?" asked Sebastian.

The exact data was ingrained in the detective's mind ever since he had read the on-the-scene officer's report. He said, "The collision happened at 1:32 p.m. and the coroner pronounced the victim dead at 1:50 p.m."

"My employee can vouch that we saw Zabel leave our parking lot soon after 12:30."

"Good. Now please tell me where you were from 1:00 p.m. to 1:30 p.m. on Monday the 3rd?"

"That's easy to remember. I went to my gallery soon after Zabel left. I got there before 1 o'clock and stayed until we closed at 4:00 p.m. We closed the gallery early because of Independence Day celebrations the next morning."

While Lieutenant Krop was typing this information into his tablet, Sebastian suddenly said, "Oh! I remember having heard sirens on Monday afternoon. The firetrucks must have rushed to the accident scene around the corner from the gallery."

"Evidently. That's all for now. I suggest you don't leave town; I may need to talk to you again."

As he got up, he remarked, "You seem to have only known Ms. Azarian by her first name. I assume you knew her before last Monday?"

"I didn't know her well but met her through her employer, who occasionally visited our gallery. As I recall, Mrs. Davenport bought some Lladro figurines from me to add to her collection."

CHAPTER 19

Zabel's funeral took place on Saturday morning, July 8, less than two weeks after the Davenports buried their mother. Derek's concept of a simple and quick occasion won, which made sense since they were unable to contact any of her friends.

Ava had called Lilly's number, listed in the ledger Zabel left behind, daily since Monday evening, to no avail. She had apparently reached the woman's landline and each time got a recording to leave a number, which she did. According to that ledger, Zabel had had no other friends. Nobody gave a eulogy and there was no memorial service.

Lieutenant Krop watched the assembled at the cremation from a distance in the hope of meeting a new suspect, but he was out of luck. Only the Davenport clan and Bonita Robles were in attendance.

Bonita was the only one shedding a tear and the family took her out to lunch after the event. The housekeeper seemed ill at ease and there was little conversation during the meal. Nobody wanted dessert, but Bonita finally warmed to the family over coffee.

Derek decided it was time to feel her out and asked, "Were you and Zabel close?"

"Not really. She was a private person, but I liked her. She took good care of Mrs. Davenport, which made me happy."

Bonita had good command of the English language but spoke with a slight accent. Her mannerism became foreign, though, as she shook a finger at him and added, "Your mother was a special lady," while tears welled up in her eyes.

He gave her time to collect herself and then said, "We learned from Mom's financial advisor that she was generous toward Zabel and you."

"Oh yes! More than generous. My husband put that money into a college fund for our two kids. They'll be the first in the family to get a higher education."

Derek pried further and inquired, "Did Zabel confide in you about any secret she kept?"

"Secret? I know nothing about a secret," said Bonita. And the irises of her dark-brown eyes suddenly expanded as she asked, "She was killed because of a secret?"

"We don't know for sure but it's possible."

"*Madre de Dios!*" exclaimed Bonita, then crossed herself immediately.

Margo thought it was best to change the subject and said, "I'm sure you're aware that my mother-in-law kept a nice wardrobe. None of us in the family are close to her size but you are. Would you like to browse through it and choose what you'd want?"

"I'd be honored," said Bonita, her composure restored.

Elliot put in, "And while you're at it, you might be able to use some stuff we found in the attic, like luggage or Christmas decorations."

Derek said, "I know I told you that the house doesn't need cleaning until it is up for sale, but since so many of us are currently living in it, it could use some vacuuming and dusting. Are you available this coming Monday the 10th?"

"I'll be there at nine o'clock," the housekeeper said.

Derek was the only one going to the auction in the afternoon. The rest of the clan were not interested. As Elliot put it, "Sebastian will credit us with the total amount of the goods. I don't need to be present when each item is being sold."

CHAPTER 20

On Sunday night, Ava and Julius parked their car near the Festival of Arts grounds and walked over to the outdoor amphitheater. Ava had purchased tickets to the *Pageant of the Masters* production in advance, securing seats at Loge Center.

The event started at 8:30 on that pleasantly warm evening. They got to their seats fifteen minutes early and Julius asked, "What exactly is this about?"

"We are going to be treated to *tableaux vivants* of classical and contemporary works of art," Ava replied.

"Speak English!"

"*Tableaux vivants* are living pictures, meaning that real people pose as the persons in the paintings. In other words, they re-create famous works of art. Mostly volunteers audition to be in the show. It is amazing what makeup, headpieces, costumes and so forth can do to make each human presentation true to its original."

"I take it that you've seen this before?"

"More than once, but each production is different."

At this point the curtain went up and it was showtime. The audience did not only get to watch "living and breathing" masterpieces but received an education on art as the evening progressed. A narrator guided them through the story of each "living" work of art on stage.

As Leonardo Da Vinci's *The Last Supper* came alive, even stoic Julius took in his breath in awe.

Ava whispered, "Told you it is breathtaking."

The last half hour was dedicated to 19th Century paintings in the style of realism. The stage lit up as two portraits came into view. The one on the left showed a young woman, almost still a girl, and the one on the right was its counterpart, a young man with his hand raised in a greeting.

A barely audible cry escaped Ava, as the narrator announced, *"Here is a pair of oil on canvas paintings, portraits of a young couple, newly engaged."*

Julius whispered, "Are you okay?"

"I'll tell you later," she muttered.

The narrator continued, *"The artist is Franz Lutzer, a realist painter, and the works are titled 'Betrothed I' and 'Betrothed II', respectively. He finished the portraits in 1855, shortly before his death. His oil on canvas works are much in demand to this day - - -"*

Ava was not listening, she just stared. The rest of the show was a blur to her as she could not get the images of *Betrothed I and Betrothed II* out of her mind.

On the short drive home Julius said, "That was amazing! A wonderful two hours spent. I truly enjoyed myself. And we got a lesson in art to boot. But what happened to you? Did you suddenly get the hiccups toward the end of the performance?"

Ava said, "I swear Franz Lutzer's portraits of the young couple hung in Mom's living room when I came for a visit about a year ago. She obviously replaced them with two of Zabel's pastels."

"So? She must have gotten tired of them. I'm sure they were only copies."

"What if they were originals?"

"They couldn't have been or she'd have kept them. And maybe you're imagining the whole thing. It's possible that you saw those two paintings somewhere else, in a museum for example."

At that point they had arrived back at the Davenport residence, but the issue of the missing paintings would not leave Ava in peace.

Julius was already in bed and she was brushing her hair when she burst out, "Think about it! If Mom was in possession of the two original Lutzer paintings, they'd be worth a small fortune. What if she made them part of her "finders keepers" joke?"

"That's insane!"

Ava stated, "You didn't know her, but I can imagine that she'd get a kick out of playing that game, knowing that we'd eventually figure it out."

Turning off the light, Ava could not see the expression on his face as he said, "And if not, Zabel knew where to look."

Julius was already snoring when Ava finally remarked, "But if those paintings really were hanging on the wall, I can't believe one of us would kill for them."

CHAPTER 21

Bonita Robles arrived promptly at 9 o'clock on Monday morning. Fifteen minutes later, Lieutenant Krop showed up unexpectedly as she was mopping the kitchen floor.

The detective apologized for the intrusion but wanted to make sure the entire household was present, since he needed to talk with each person separately. He went back to his car twice to fetch Zabel's belongings that had been salvaged from the totaled car, including her pastel paintings.

He said, "We could not locate any next of kin for Zabel Azarian, so I'm leaving her possessions with you for now. Maybe with time you can find a relative of hers that lives abroad. As for her artwork, I understand that it used to hang in this house, so theoretically, it is yours."

The interviews took place in the den, starting with Derek.

Lieutenant Krop said, "When I talked to you as a group the other day, you said that you had all stayed here after lunch on Monday, July 3rd until evening. Did you, or anyone else, leave during the afternoon, no matter for how short a time?"

"I don't know about the others, but I drove my wife to our hotel because she prefers working there. I was only gone for a few minutes; the hotel is right here in town."

"At what time was that?"

"Soon after lunch. We ate around noon, so it might have been 12:20 or 12:30. I was back before 1 o'clock. Look Lieutenant, I know you're checking us for alibis, but the culprit may have been a stranger."

"No, sir, that's out of the question. The victim was drugged. You don't sit down and have a beverage with a stranger."

"I meant a stranger to us."

"That's always a possibility; I'm not ruling it out."

Derek could not hide his irritation and blurted, "How much longer is this going to take?"

"If you mean the investigation, it will take until the arrest of Zabel's killer."

"I'd like to put the house up for sale, which can't happen while the entire clan is stranded here."

"I have a lead and am counting on its merit."

Derek's alarm went off on his smart watch and he stated, "I have a conference Zoom meeting in five minutes. Are we almost done?"

"In that case, we're done for now." The lieutenant said.

Interviews with the rest of the family went more or less the same way. The majority of the suspects either stayed home the entire afternoon, or if running an errand got back within minutes. Paulette suggested suicide, but the detective set her straight by stating that the victim would not have deliberately overdosed on sleeping pills and then gotten behind the wheel. She would have either taken the pills or driven herself into the building, but not both.

He also took the opportunity to have a few words with Bonita Robles, since she was conveniently present. From her he learned that the last time she had seen Zabel Azarian was at Norma Davenport's funeral. On the day of Zabel's murder, she had been working from 10:00 a.m. until 2:00 p.m. at a residence in Del Mar, and she gave him the name and address.

When Lieutenant Krop left the Davenport residence, he was no closer to solving the case than when he had arrived. As for the siblings, they were stuck with Zabel's belongings, having no clue what to do with them. And no one wanted to keep her paintings, as they would be a constant reminder of what had happened to her.

CHAPTER 22

Minutes after the law enforcer left, the doorbell rang once more and Margo came face to face with Sebastian Brunt. He wanted to talk to the entire household, so she ushered him into the den where Stella and Ava had started to continue their task of organizing photo albums as Lieutenant Krop's last interview came to a conclusion in the den.

Ava hated to be interrupted again and exclaimed, "It's like Grand Central Station around here."

Once they had all gathered around Sebastian, he said, "I have great news. The proceeds from the auction are higher than expected. Especially the silver was in demand as two bidders wouldn't give up."

Looking at Derek he continued, "You were there and know what I'm talking about."

Derek grinned. "It was a battle to the end."

Sebastian glanced at his paperwork and stated, "The total amount for items sold at the auction was $61,000, minus my 15%, which leaves you with a nice sum of $51,850." He looked up and asked, "To whom do I make the check out?"

Elliot turned to his siblings and inquired, "Everybody okay if he makes it out to Derek? We trust him to divide it among us, right?"

Nobody objected.

✳✳✳

In the afternoon when Bonita had finished cleaning, Paulette asked her to come to the master bedroom and select whatever she wanted out of the walk-in closet, which she was more than happy to do. Elliot then escorted her up to the attic, where she chose luggage and the entire stock of Christmas decorations.

Ready to leave and on her way to the front door, Ava begged the housekeeper to come back to the living room and said, "Remember the two end-tables that used to stand here?"

"Yes, of course," said Bonita.

"And do you also remember the pictures that hung on the wall above them?"

"Sure, I remember Zabel's ocean scenes."

"I meant the two oils on canvas by Lutzer."

"You're talking about the horrible portraits of the young couple?"

"Yes. But why did you think they were horrible?"

"They gave me the shivers, is why. That young girl looked terrified. I was so glad when Mrs. Davenport got rid of them and hung the lovely ocean pictures instead."

"When was that?"

"I don't know exactly, less than a year ago."

"Do you know where those Lutzer paintings are now?"

"I have no idea. And, if you want my opinion, *good riddance!*" said Bonita.

That established, the housekeeper was finally on her way out the door. Ava helped her carry the three suitcases to her car; one containing clothing, the other two filled with Christmas decorations.

In their room that Monday night, Ava told Julius about her chat with Bonita, ending with, "So you see, I'm not imagining things!"

CHAPTER 23

Early Tuesday morning, July 11, Lieutenant Krop was sitting in his office, doing some serious thinking. His photographic memory came in handy in his profession. He remembered each suspect's interview in detail. He now thought about what he had told Derek yesterday, "I have a lead." That was a lie.

The interviews he had had proved less than productive. He went through each one in his mind's eye, then made a chart of where each family member was during the crucial time:

Derek and Elliot - attic, sorting stuff

Lucas and Julius - garage, sorting stuff

Stella and Ava - den, going through photo albums

Margo - hotel, working

Paulette - master bedroom, going through clothing. Also fourth bedroom, going through more clothing

These people all had alibis depending on one another. Derek may have been out longer than he claims when he drove his wife to the hotel, and Elliot could have left the attic and driven away during the time his brother was gone. Lucas and Julius claimed they were in the garage together, except during the short time that Julius and Ava decided they needed to get a few items from the grocery store. They could not remember exactly when that was.

Not only did husband and wife vouch for each other, but Lucas was alone in the garage while they were out and Stella was also by herself in the den. Margo was driven to her hotel at 12:20 or 12:30 and stayed there all afternoon, leaving Paulette in the master bedroom alone.

Any of those folks could have snuck out during the crucial time and driven away except for Margo, who was at the hotel with no car. And he mused, but not even Margo is cleared. Her hotel location is within a mile of where the crash happened, so she could have walked to a rendezvous with Zabel.

As for persons outside the family, Sebastian Brunt was at his gallery, either in the showroom or in his office, from 12:50p.m. until closing time at 4:00 p.m. He was seen there not only by several employees, but also by clients.

Bonita Robles had an airtight alibi as well. She had been cleaning a house in Del Mar from 10:00 a.m. until 2:00 p.m. on Monday, July 3, verified by her Del Mar employer.

He considered further, the person noted in Zabel's ledger by the name of Lilly was a long shot. At the beginning of the investigation he had dialed her number but got a recording to leave a message, which he did. He had called again yesterday, with the same result and no return call. He had then pulled his "authority muscle" and was informed by the telephone company that the number was a landline and belonged to someone in Arcadia.

He shook his head. If this Lilly, whose last name was unknown to him, was a friend of Zabel, he could not imagine why she would not return a call from a police officer, which must have sounded alarming. The message he had left was, "I have urgent information about Zabel Azarian." He muttered to himself, "I'm giving you the benefit of a doubt, lady. After all, it's July and you might be on vacation."

The detective sighed and thought, it stands to reason that one of the family must be the culprit, but for the life of me I can't come up with a motive for any one of them. There are generally three basic motives for murder: Greed, passion, or self-preservation. Zabel was the late Norma Davenport's companion. None of these people profit from her death. A crime of passion is also out of the question. And as far as self-preservation, he did not believe that Zabel was a threat to any of them; they hardly knew her.

He flipped through the autopsy report once more. The medical jargon aside, what it came down to was that due to the car's frontal collision with the building, the victim suffered multiple internal hemorrhages. In other words, she bled to death. Besides the sleeping pills, the stomach contents showed partly digested bacon, eggs, and toast - - an indication that she had consumed breakfast but not lunch.

The lieutenant also browsed through the information he had from the forensics team. No useful clues were found in the car. The only DNA on the victim's body was her own. There was a fresh stain on her blouse, which was identified as lemonade.

Then he tried to reconstruct Zabel's movements after she had left the auction house at 12:30 p.m.

She must have met someone within the next hour or, more likely, within the next half hour. That someone must have felt threatened by her and lured her to a meeting, then slipped sleeping pills into her drink, which would have taken effect in only a few minutes. Most likely, that beverage would have been lemonade, ergo the fresh stain on Zabel's blouse. The rendezvous could have been in a restaurant, coffee shop, the park, or anywhere else in Laguna Beach.

The only location it could not have taken place was at the Davenport residence. Zabel would have been unable to meet the villain there without any of the others noticing. She certainly could not have parked her car in the garage without either Lucas or Julius being aware of it. Besides, she would have had to drive off again in order to crash her car, which made no sense.

He stamped his foot in frustration and thought, this is not getting me anywhere. And he admitted to himself that the biggest problem was motive. As far as he knew, none of these suspects had had reason to kill Zabel Azarian.

CHAPTER 24

In the next few days, there was a general mood of discord among the Davenport household ever since their individual interviews had taken place with Lieutenant Krop. Everyone became aware that there may be a killer among them, which they found hard to believe but made them suspicious of one another nonetheless.

Margo spent most of her days at the hotel, maintaining it was because of work deadlines. Although true, that was no longer her main reason for staying away from the house; she felt safer at the hotel.

The rest looked at each other sideways and some were jumpy as a wild colt. Stella, especially, was a bundle of nerves. Startled when one of her brothers came into a room close behind her, she panicked and screamed. Derek threw himself even more into his job than normal - - he was either on the phone or his computer nonstop - - which seemed to distract him from their current plight. Paulette became a recluse, staying in the master bedroom, except for meals. The only one who still joked around was Elliot. That may have been his way of dealing with their predicament.

By Friday, July 14, the tension between siblings and their spouses had become unbearable. Derek had called the night before, asking everyone to stay put the next morning, as they needed to discuss the situation.

During the short drive from their hotel to the Davenport house, Margo asked, "Why are you making me come along? I don't know anything about what happened to Zabel, so I won't be of any use."

"That's not the point," Derek stated. "We need to decide on how to proceed. If it comes to casting votes, we all need to be present."

"What are we voting about?"

"You'll see," he replied.

At that point they had arrived at the house and he parked his white Mercedes-Benz on the circular driveway.

Making his siblings and their spouses gather in the den for discussions had become routine to Derek.

He started by saying, "That Lieutenant Krop is dragging his feet. By now he should be solving the case, but we haven't heard from him since he was here on Monday."

Elliot said, "I'm sure he's working on it. What makes you think he owes us a report?"

Derek was tongue-tied for the first time in his life. The idea that the detective was not obligated to inform them of his progress had not occurred to him.

Elliot grinned and stated, "Aha! You're not used to being ignored. Give yourself a rest, you're not the CEO here."

Derek overlooked his brother's remark and continued, "Whether or not we are kept in the dark, to my knowledge, the lieutenant has not questioned anyone further, nor has he made an arrest. In my opinion, the man is incompetent."

"Why do you think so?" asked Paulette

"From the beginning, I thought that Zabel was killed by an outsider, and that is still my belief. But it looks like the detective in charge is determined to pin the crime on one of us."

Julius asked, "Did you call us to the den to let us know what you think of Lieutenant Krop, or does your meeting have another purpose?"

Derek shot him an angry glance and said, "I was getting to that. I suggest we hire a private investigator."

There was a moment of silence, then everyone talked at once, but it did not look like most took to the idea. The general opinion was that a private eye would have nothing further to go on than the lieutenant.

Elliot said, "Private eyes don't come cheap. Are you willing to pay for one?"

"I'm suggesting that we all chip in. That would only be fair."

Hearing that, the group was even less enthused about the idea, but Derek insisted on taking votes.

As expected, Derek voted "yes." Margo's vote was also a "yes" in support of her husband. Ava had her own reason for a "yes" vote. All others voted "no."

Derek announced, "Three yes's and five no's. Looks like I'm outvoted. We may all regret this but at least I tried. Now we are at the mercy of the lieutenant for solving the case in a speedy manner."

Elliot grinned and said, "If you're done with your agenda, I have a proposal too."

"Go ahead."

"How about taking advantage of our situation by indulging in a little gambling? I'll volunteer as your bookie. We write down the name of the person we think killed Zabel, back it up with a little bet money, and toss it in a hat. Once the investigation is over and the case solved, the winner collects."

Lucas, who had not spoken more than two words to the group in days, pointed an accusing finger at Elliot and declared, "You are not funny!"

CHAPTER 25

Ava hadn't been able to get the Lutzer paintings out of her head. On Friday afternoon, she sat in that fourth bedroom, which had become her "home away from home", trying to take care of some online banking but could not concentrate. Her eyes left the screen and she thought back to the conversation she'd had with Bonita.

Strange how the housekeeper had called the portraits horrible and thought the young woman in *Betrothed I* looked terrified. When Ava reflected on the presentation of the two portraits of the live reproduction at the *Pageant of the Masters,* and also seeing the paintings hanging on her mother's living room wall during her visit, she did not get the impression that the young woman looked scared, certainly not terrified. Yes, there were no smiles on either the woman or the man, but posing for a portrait in the 19th Century was a serious matter. Serene was the expression on their faces, as far as Ava remembered.

Her thoughts then strayed to the suggestion Derek had made that morning. Would a private investigator be of help to find out what Mom did with the paintings? Ava hadn't told anyone what she'd discovered, so except for

Julius, nobody knew about *Betrothed I and Betrothed II's* existence.

I take that back, she told herself, Zabel's killer may not only know, but also know where to look for them. Since the majority of the family was against hiring a private eye, she didn't want to go behind their backs and engage one on her own. She would do the sleuthing herself, she concluded.

For the next few minutes she forced herself to focus back on her laptop and finish the started banking business. With that task accomplished, she got creative.

First, she called Miles Rotterdam, her mom's estate lawyer. After a couple of telephone tags - - his secretary was screening incoming calls - - she finally got the attorney on the line. Following the initial greeting, their conversation went like this:

Ava: *"Did my mom confide in you about assets in addition to what she said in her video?"*

Rotterdam: *"I don't follow. What is your question?"*

Ava: *"From her video we learned that the four of us siblings inherit the house and that the rest is 'finders keepers,' as she put it. Did she ever mention to you that she invested some of her money in artwork?"*

Rotterdam: *"Mrs. Vazquez! I was your mother's estate lawyer. As such I drew up her will and living trust according to her wishes, but I was and am in the dark about her assets. Estate lawyers do not obtain information about their clients' finances."*

Ava: *"I understand but thought that she might have confided in you about an investment of famous paintings."*

Rotterdam: *"What you learned from the video and its counterpart of the written will is exactly what I know of your mother's assets."*

Ava had not expected to get much useful information from the lawyer but was disappointed, nonetheless when they ended the call. Next, she tackled Earl Silverton, her mom's tax guy and financial advisor.

The phone conversation with Mr. Silverton went along the same line as the one she had had with Miles Rotterdam but was even shorter.

When asked if he knew anything about her mom's investment in any artwork, he said, "Like I told your brother and sister the other day, your mother came to me two years ago demanding that I terminate all her investments. She gave $100,000 to her companion and $50,000 to her housekeeper. What she did with the rest of her money is a mystery to me. And like I told your siblings, I tried my best to make her change her mind, but she was determined to walk away with cash. After that day, I was no longer your mother's financial advisor and had not heard from her since."

As they ended the call Ava thought, so much for my brilliant idea. Nobody knew anything then nor knows anything now. I have to look at things from a different angle. She tried to put herself into her mom's frame of mind from two years ago. Learning of her heart condition and opting not to have surgery must have made an impact on her outlook on life.

Making the cash gifts to Zabel and Bonita was an indication that she thought she could die at any moment. Purchasing the two Lutzer paintings may have been a luxury she treated herself to at that point. They may have hung in her living room for her to enjoy for about a year. After all, I saw them there last year.

Then, when she came up with her joke of making us 'work' for our inheritance of jewelry, et cetera, she had fun imagining how we would search for the remainder of her belongings. So the switch with Zabel's pastels took place. Now, where would she have stashed the two oils on canvas by Lutzer? You can't hide paintings easily, she reflected.

Ava was sure her mom did not sell the artwork. She meant for her children to have it, or at least for the one who'd find it. Did the person who killed Zabel already know where to look? she wondered. She assumed that all others had not even seen the paintings in their mom's living room, and if they did, they must have thought them copies, not originals. She herself had initially assumed that. Maybe I should drop the bombshell and watch their reactions. But first, I need to find out what the portraits are worth, she mused.

Googling it proved a waste of time. She could not get a price on the portraits but offers of other paintings by art collectors and galleries were abundant. In the end, she made a third phone call. This one to Sebastian Brunt.

Ava inquired, "Can you give me a ballpark figure of how much original paintings by Franz Lutzer are worth?"

Sebastian replied, "Franz Lutzer's works have appreciated in the last few years, especially his oil on canvases. Can you be more specific? Lutzer is famous for his landscapes but has done still lifes and a few portraits too."

"I'm interested in *Betrothed I and II.*"

There was a pause on the line, then Sebastian said, "Wow! You pick the frontrunner. The artist died shortly after completing the pair of portraits, so they are among his most in demand. Why are you interested in *Betrothed I and Betrothed II* ?"

Ava decided not to take him into her confidence and said, "I saw them at the *Pageant of the Masters* production the other night and thought they were fascinating."

"You should have mentioned 'spoiler alert'! I haven't seen this year's show yet but have tickets for next weekend."

"I'm sorry about that but how much are the paintings worth?"

"Give me a couple minutes and I'll do the research," he said.

It took him less than two minutes to get back to her and he stated, "They're in the $175,000 range each. Are you interested in acquiring them?"

"Not at that price. I was mainly curious and you satisfied my curiosity. Thank you so much." she said.

After ending the call Ava thought, I was right. Since the portraits are worth $350,000, that amount makes up most of the missing assets.

Sebastian for his part thought, that sure was a strange request. What, exactly, was she fishing for?

CHAPTER 26

Lieutenant Krop also opted to consult the art collector once more but on a different matter. He had been trying to trace Zabel's movements on her last day again. What if the killer had not arranged for a rendezvous but had followed her from the auction house and approached her at a destination she had chosen to stop. Say, a restaurant or a grocery store with an opportunity to sit down and consume a beverage?

The detective visited the Brunt Gallery where Sebastian spent most of his time, unless he was preparing for an auction. Lt. Krop had driven by the gallery and even walked by countless times but had never ventured inside. There were only a few interested people in the place when he entered, which was surprising for an end-of-the-week afternoon.

He was no art connoisseur but was impressed by the large display of works. He stood and viewed a landscape pencil drawing in black and white. The sketch portrayed a chalet by a river in the foreground and enormous mountain peaks in the distance. The tranquil scene reminded him of a spot he had rested at while hiking in the Swiss alps when on a trip in Europe.

"May I help you?" said a young woman who had appeared out of nowhere and was no doubt in charge.

"Is Sebastian Brunt in?" asked the lieutenant.

"He is, but I can answer any question you may have."

"I'm sure you can but this is an official matter," he replied and showed his badge.

"Oh, she said," and looked around to make certain that no one else had seen him show his credential. Then she nodded, "This way, please," and led him to her boss's office, situated to the side of the gallery at the back entrance.

Sebastian was on the phone when the lieutenant stood at the open door but motioned him in and pointed to a chair across from his desk and then ended the call.

"Sorry, I didn't mean to interrupt," said the lieutenant.

"No problem, I was done," Sebastian assured him. "But if you're here about poor Zabel, I told you all I know."

"I'm sure you did. I just have an additional question. Last time we talked, you said that you and your employee saw Zabel Azarian drive out of your auction house's rear parking lot."

"That's correct. We did."

"In the meantime, I gave that back parking lot a closer look. There are only five spaces. Did you see any other cars parked there on Monday, July 3rd, around 12:30 p.m., besides Zabel's Tesla?"

Sebastian thought about it and then said, "My employee had parked our company truck in the back, and my Lexus was there too. So that makes only three cars, including Zabel's, that were parked in our small lot at that time."

"How about on the street, overlooking your mini lot?"

"I happened to glance that way and saw a car parked at the curb."

"What make was that?"

Sebastian closed his eyes, trying to call to mind what he had seen. He opened them and said, "It may have been a Mercedes, but I can't be sure."

"What color?"

"A light color but I can't be specific. I really didn't pay much attention at the time."

"Was the car vacant or did someone sit at the wheel?"

He closed his eyes again and then recalled, "I'm almost positive someone sat in the driver seat reading the paper."

Lieutenant Krop said, "Thanks. That's the only question I had."

He got up and looked out the window and remarked, "How convenient. You have a back parking lot here too, practically at the doorstep of your gallery."

"It sure comes in handy when people pick up their purchases."

The detective was already at the door when Sebastian said, "Sorry I wasn't able to be of more help."

"You've helped quite a bit," replied the detective.

Out the front door and on his way to the car, he thought, I have my theory now, but that's all it is. No real evidence. Everything is circumstantial and I still cannot come up with a motive.

CHAPTER 27

Ava called everyone to the den in the late afternoon of that same Friday and stated, "For once Derek is not calling the shots but I'm the one who has the floor. And you'd better pay attention to what I have to say."

She stared them down and continued, "Our scavenger hunt is no longer fun and games. Mom had no idea that her joke would bring out the worst in us. I bet she is appalled by looking at us from wherever she's at, realizing that one of us is a murderer. And for $350,000 to be exact. Shame on you!"

Pointing an accusing finger at Derek, she continued, "I overheard one of your phone conversations and know that you're in financial distress."

She glared at the rest of people in the room and stated, "Don't tell me the thought of living in this wonderful house and being able to buy the others out hasn't occurred to all of us."

Several voiced their protest but she held up both arms to silence them and said, "I've done my homework. *Betrothed I and Betrothed II* are worth $175,000 each."

She watched them carefully when mentioning the paintings but there was no reaction from her audience. Not even a flicker of an eyelid or an intake of breath.

Margo said, "I have no idea what you're talking about. What is betrothed one and two?"

Ava replied, "For those of you who are in the dark, Betrothed Roman numerals I and II is a pair of portraits, painted by Franz Lutzer. They hung in our mom's living room until they were replaced by Zabel's works."

Now there were expressions of surprise on some of their faces but not the countenance she was looking for.

While addressing the entire group but hoping that one person would feel singled out, she continued, "Did Zabel give you the info willingly about where Mom was hiding those works of art, or did she put up a fight before you drugged her?"

Elliot burst out, "Now hold on! Do you have proof for your blatant accusation?"

Ava kept her cool and remarked, "It's good to know that you're no longer treating our situation as a comedy. To answer your question, I can get the proof."

That said, she turned and marched out the door. After a moment of hesitation, Julius followed her.

The rest stayed put in the den, stunned.

Derek was the first to recover and said, "Our baby sister has gone off the deep end. She has lost her mind or, at the very least, has a wild imagination."

"What about those paintings that she claims Mom had?" asked Stella.

"All fabrication of her mind. I never saw them in the house or knew of them. And now that we've gone through everything in the entire place, including the attic, there is no trace of them, as far as I'm aware."

Stella persisted, "But if it's true, the $350,000 Ava mentioned would about cover the lost amount of our inheritance. The artwork could be stored at a different location."

Nobody commented further, but they all secretly decided to watch their backs from now on as they filed out of their mother's den.

CHAPTER 28

On their drive to dinner at Sebastian's house, Elliot remarked, "A change of pace will do you good. You've been letting our current situation overwhelm you."

"Maybe. But it's not going to change anything," Paulette replied.

"True, but for a couple of hours we can forget our troubles and enjoy ourselves."

As they pulled into the Brunts' driveway, he said, "I didn't realize his house was so close to Mom's, we could have walked."

They were greeted by Sebastian, who ushered them into the dining room, while Carla tended to last minute tasks in the kitchen.

Their salads were already served at each of their table settings, and Sebastian opened a bottle of Chianti.

Carla carried in a steaming dish of lasagna and said, "Sorry it's not veal piccata. I know that's Elliot's favorite, but veal is impossible to find these days."

The lasagna was prepared to perfection and enjoyed by all. Their conversation was lighthearted during the meal, the main topics being the play Carla had been participating in at the Laguna Playhouse and the trip to Hawaii the Brunts had taken in the spring.

It was only over a light dessert of mango sherbet that the dreaded subject came up.

Sebastian asked, "How is the investigation of Zabel's case coming along?"

Elliot answered, "As far as the authorities go, we are kept in the dark but that doesn't mean that the detective in charge, Lieutenant Krop, is idle. I have the feeling that he's very much in control."

"I've met the lieutenant and agree. He's sharp."

"On the other hand, my sister Ava was out of control today."

He looked at Paulette and said, "Shall I tell them?"

She shrugged her shoulders, knowing that he was going to do so whether she agreed or not.

After a slight pause Elliot told their friends about the speech Ava had given in the den that afternoon.

When he came to a halt, Sebastian said, "Now I know what that phone call was about."

"What phone call?"

"Ava called out of the blue and wanted to know what the paintings by Franz Lutzer, *Betrothed I and Betrothed II*, were worth. She said the two portraits were in this year's *Pageant of the Masters*, which I now know is a fact. Carla and I will not see the show until tomorrow, but I was able to get a hold of a program. Still, I thought the request about the value of the portraits was a strange one and guessed that she must have an ulterior motive for asking. Well, now it makes sense!"

"So those paintings are going for $175,000 each, just like she said?"

"In that range, yes."

"And they actually exist and belonged to Mom, except we have no idea where they are hidden?"

Sebastian stated, "They do exist, but I don't know if your mother was ever in possession of them."

Paulette got into the conversation and said, "So we don't know if Ava was telling the truth or if she made the whole thing up."

"Sounds far-fetched to me if she invented a story like that," said Carla, "but then, I haven't met Ava and don't know what she's like."

Elliot stated, "If she was on the level with her accusation, it looks to me like she'd only fished for a reaction and has no clue who the culprit is."

Sebastian had the last word and said, "In any event, your sister is playing a dangerous game."

CHAPTER 29

Early on Saturday morning Ava got up, donned a pair of jogging shorts with a matching t-shirt, and laced up her running sneakers. A shower would have to wait until her return. She tip-toed by their bed as Julius, a light sleeper, opened his eyes and asked, "Seven o'clock already?"

"A quarter to. I'm a bit early today," she replied. "Go back to sleep."

She descended the stairs to the kitchen, poured herself a cup of instant coffee, and nibbled on a handful of trail mix. Then she was out the door.

Ava had established a route for her daily early morning jogs ever since arriving in town three weeks ago. Only three weeks, she thought to herself. It seemed like an eternity. The half-hour run took her through a residential neighborhood, with mostly flat terrain, except for one small hill, which she conquered by slowing down to a fast walk only.

As a rule, she did not do much thinking when jogging but concentrated on her breathing. On that day, though, she could not help herself. Her mind was stuck on the confrontation she had had the previous day with her siblings and their spouses. What a disappointment! She had counted on someone's reaction, but there had been none. Whoever is the guilty person sure kept a perfect poker face throughout, she mused.

Ava had a hard time accepting the fact that one of the family was capable of murder. A week ago, she was sure that it must have been an outsider who killed Zabel. What she had learned on the evening they attended the *Pageant of the Masters* changed everything.

So what now? Julius had told her to leave it alone. She did not understand how he could be so untouched by it all.

When she came to a curve on the sidewalk, just before the uphill part, her mind was made up. She'd call Lieutenant Krop first thing Monday morning. He didn't know about the Lutzer paintings and she thought it was time he knew.

"Hey, Ava! Wait up," someone behind her shouted.

Alert, she turned her head.

"Oh, it's you," she said and relaxed.

Letting the other person catch up, she jogged in place. When the two were side by side, she asked, "What are you - - -"

Too late she realized the danger as two hands grabbed her neck and squeezed. She was taken by total surprise and had no chance to reach for the whistle she carried in her pocket. She tried to scream and at the same time kick the person in the groin, but only a gurgle escaped her and her leg barely touched the other's knee. Her struggle was over within seconds as her body became limp. The last thought before she lost consciousness was, *I should have guessed.*

Her attacker kept the pressure up for another minute, to make sure she was no longer breathing. Then the person let her crumple to the ground and shoved her into a bush next to the sidewalk, in order to hide her corpse from plain view.

The culprit then turned and briskly walked away, knowing that at that early hour on Saturday chances were slim of encountering anyone else in the strictly domestic neighborhood.

Three hours later, two boys discovered Ava's body when the ball they kicked around rolled into the bush her lifeless form was under.

CHAPTER 30

Lieutenant Krop needed to interview each family member again, pertaining to Ava's murder. This time he asked them to come to the police station, first thing Monday morning, where he made them sit and sweat until called into the interrogation room, one by one.

He had the autopsy report stored in his mind. It was simple and to the point. Death by manual strangulation. The coroner had examined the corpse at 10:27 and estimated that death had occurred three to three-and-a-half hours prior. In the lieutenant's approximation that pinned the murder between 7:00 and 7:30 a.m.

He had also taken a Sunday morning stroll through the neighborhood and timed the scene of the crime to 15 minutes away from the Davenport residence on foot. If driven, the time was under a minute.

Julius was first. The room itself was intimidating. The only furniture were two chairs facing one another across a small table. A bright light from above shone directly at the person being questioned. The rest of the room was kept dimmed.

Julius was shaken, no doubt; whether by grief or being intimidated by his surroundings was unclear.

The lieutenant began with some generic questions, like date of birth, home address, phone number, and other basic data. Then he said, "Mr. Vazquez, how long have you been married to Ava Vazquez?"

"Three months."

"You were practically newlyweds, then."

"Yes, I'm new to the family," he stammered, "but they're starting to give me the creeps."

"We'll get to that later. Let's first finish with your profile. You've been married before, correct?"

Julius could not disguise the anger in his voice as he said, "You've obviously checked me out. Yes, I'm divorced."

"And your first wife pays you alimony, that's also correct?"

"Since you are so well informed, you must know that she's the one making the big bucks and she was the one who cheated on me, not the other way around. On top of that, she was the one filing for divorce."

Now that the lieutenant had his suspect all steamed up, he continued, "Let's establish the facts. Where were you on Saturday, July 15, from 6:45 a.m. until 7:45 a.m.?"

"In bed, asleep," Julius shot back.

"You did not hear your wife get up?" the detective asked, raising a brow.

"I did hear her and asked what time it was, but went back to sleep."

"So at what time did she leave?"

"I don't know exactly, but she said it was a quarter to seven as she left the room."

"I don't follow. Did she or didn't she go on her jog at 6:45?"

Julius got flustered and said, "She had a routine by going down to the kitchen and having coffee before going on her runs. She may have left closer to seven, but I don't know. Like I said, I fell back asleep."

"And going for a jog was her routine of how often?"

"Every day, no exceptions."

The lieutenant leaned forward and sounded almost friendly as he inquired, "You said earlier that the Davenport family is giving you the creeps. Be more specific."

"Obviously, they're after the missing assets that their late mother left behind, and one of them did not hesitate to kill Zabel for the information. And now that my wife forced the person's hand, she was murdered too. I told her to leave it alone, but my Ava could be stubborn." He looked away from the lieutenant, trying to hide the tears that were welling up.

Pretending not to notice, the detective asked, "What missing assets?"

"At first we thought it was money, or at least documents that would show how the funds were allocated, but then Ava figured out that her mom had invested the assets in valuable paintings."

"Your statement doesn't make sense to me. Explain it, step by step."

Julius hesitated for a second but then told the entire story, from A to Z. He started with explaining the strange game the late Norma Davenport had played about *finders keepers* when setting up her will. He continued with informing the lieutenant of Norma's missing assets of over $350,000 and of Zabel's apparent knowledge about where to find them. He then talked about Ava's discovery of the Franz Lutzer paintings, and finally of her provocation meeting with the family the day before she was strangled.

There was a long pause while Lieutenant Krop stored all that information into his photographic memory.

He finally said, "I wish your wife would have come to me with her findings and not played at amateur detecting. Chances are that I couldn't have prevented her death, but by God I would have tried."

Julius was excused and, as he left the interrogation room, wondered if it was wise to tell Lieutenant Krop the entire story. He thought, I probably shouldn't have but had no choice. I don't owe that family a thing.

CHAPTER 31

Although the interrogation room made most uncomfortable, Lieutenant Krop did not learn anything new from questioning the next several suspects. Stella appeared especially jumpy, but the lieutenant attributed that to her tense disposition.

When he asked the crucial question, "Where were you on Saturday, July 15, from 6:45 a.m. until 7:45 a.m.?" he got more or less the same answer. According to the whole household, all were either still asleep or had gone down to the kitchen for breakfast.

Nobody had left the house, neither by car or on foot. This was vouched for by spouses or other members of the family. Margo swore that she and Derek slept in and had not left their hotel room during that hour.

Granted, it was early in the morning on a weekend. On the surface, it looked like they were telling the truth. But again, like in Zabel Azarian's case, their alibis depended on one another in Ava's strangulation.

To his inquiry of whether people knew about Ava's jogging habit, all replied in the affirmative. Not only did they know that she went for a run every morning at approximately the same time, but she had also told them about her route early on in their stay at Laguna Beach.

The lieutenant purposely left Derek for last. Let him stew a little, he decided. If he was correct in his assessment, Derek Davenport was the type of person who did not like to be kept waiting.

CHAPTER 32

By the time Derek was escorted to the interrogation room, he was about to explode with pent up emotion but outwardly managed to look controlled. When he sat facing an empty chair across the small table, and realized that he was made to wait again, he almost lost his temper. He had seen enough TV crime shows to assume that he was being watched, so he folded his hands together and forced them to rest in his lap.

Minutes later, when the lieutenant showed up and sat down facing him, Derek's voice was controlled as he said, "I am trying not to be insulted. As the first born and head of the family, common courtesy would have put me first, not last."

"You've got that all wrong," Lieutenant Krop assured him. "Keeping you last helps me determine whether the other suspects made accurate statements."

The little buttering up worked, keeping Derek compliant when answering the lieutenant's generic questions for the record. When asked about his whereabouts at the crucial time on Saturday morning, July 15, his answer was as expected. He and Margo had been together in their hotel room.

Suddenly the interrogation turned aggressive when the detective prompted, "I learned from another suspect about the missing paintings by Franz Lutzer. How come you, as the head of the family, did not inform me about that?"

"Hold on! Ava told us about those alleged paintings only on Friday. To tell the truth, I thought she had made them up. I never saw any works by Lutzer hanging in my mother's living room."

The lieutenant glared at him and said, "But you knew about their existence and possibly where to find them. You killed twice to safeguard your secret."

Derek stared. Then he burst out, "I didn't know and certainly am not the killer!"

"I have a witness that puts you and your white Mercedes on the street overlooking the Brunt auction house's back parking lot on Monday, July 3rd at around 12:30 p.m. A reminder, that was the day that Zabel Azarian was murdered."

There was a sharp intake of breath and Derek shook his head in frustration and then said, "It looks bad but - - -"

"Are you denying being there at that time and then following Zabel when she drove off?"

"I was there but didn't follow her. I can explain."

"You'd better!"

"It's embarrassing."

"You have to worry about much more than embarrassment."

So Derek told his story. "I had just dropped Margo off at the hotel and was on the return drive to the house via the back road when I saw Zabel's Tesla parked in Brunt's lot. On the spur of the moment I decided to wait for her to question her about Mom's missing funds. I suspected that Zabel knew more than she led us to believe. I admit that I'm in a bit of a financial bind and wanted to talk to her without the others' knowledge. I'm not proud of that, but that's what I had in mind."

He swallowed empty and then continued, "While waiting, I suddenly felt foolish and decided to forget it. I was about to drive away when Zabel came out the back door with Sebastian and another person, who helped load her paintings into the trunk of her car. After she drove off, I left too and went straight to the house. I swear to God that I never followed her. All I had in mind was to talk with her, and I didn't even do that."

Lieutenant Krop had been hoping for a confession but not the kind he received. Whether he believed the man was irrelevant. The issue being that, although he finally was aware of a motive, pinning the homicide on Derek with only circumstantial evidence was not going to happen.

He asked, "Why didn't you mention any of this during my initial round of questioning?"

"It was embarrassing, and I didn't think it mattered."

"Is there anything *embarrassing* you forgot to mention about your sister's jog on Saturday, between the hour of 6:45 a.m. and 7:45 a.m.?"

"I swear to having never left the hotel during that time," said Derek.

The lieutenant looked him in the eye and stated, "If that is true, you have nothing to worry about."

And after a pause, which made Derek moist under the armpits, he added, "You are free to go, but let me stress again, *don't leave town*."

CHAPTER 33

As they drove away from the police station Margo asked, "Did you tell him about leaving the hotel room on Saturday morning when you went down to the lobby for the continental breakfast?"

"No. Did you?"

"I told him we were together in our room at the time in question, but I realized as soon as I said it that my statement wasn't accurate. You were gone for breakfast for a short time," said Margo.

"That's none of the lieutenant's business. And anyhow, what difference does it make? I stayed in the hotel the entire time. You know that. I even brought your breakfast back to our room."

"Oh, there is no doubt in my mind. I only want to make sure that we told the same story."

"It's not a story. As far as I'm concerned, it's the truth."

They drove the rest of the short way in silence, each preoccupied in dealing with their own thoughts.

***

Earlier in the day, Elliot and Paulette had had a similar conversation in their car.

Paulette asked, "Did you tell the lieutenant that you went to buy the paper early in the morning?"

"I'd forgotten all about it and when I did remember, I didn't think it was a good idea to change my statement. Why? Did you tell him?"

"No. I didn't think it was important. You were only gone for a few minutes. But it was a mistake. We should have told him. What if one of the others mentioned it? Some were in the kitchen fixing breakfast when you announced that you were getting the paper."

"I have nothing to hide, so don't worry about it. I kept the paper; if necessary, I can show it as proof of my alibi," he joked.

***

In bed that night after turning off the light, Stella was about to dose off when Lucas asked, "Are you awake?"

Her husband rarely started a conversation, especially not late at night. On the rare occasions that he did have something to say, Stella paid attention.

She said, "What's up?"

"Where were you early Saturday morning?"

"What do you mean?"

"I took a quick shower after you left the room and minutes later, when I came down to the kitchen, you were not there. As I was done with my breakfast, you showed up and had yours. I thought nothing of it at the time, but started wondering about it after what happened to Ava."

Stella sat straight up in bed and cried out, "I can't believe you think I had anything to do with Ava's death!"

"Of course I don't. I'd just like to know where you were."

"For your information, you doubting Thomas, I was in the den. I had been thinking back to Ava's speech about the artwork she'd been talking about and an idea suddenly occurred to me. Was it possible that Mom hinted where those paintings could be found in her last will and testament communication? So I went in search of that flash drive and inserted it into the TV. I listened to the video twice to make sure I didn't miss anything."

She lay back down, turned on her side away from him, and added, "Now you know where I was and what I was doing. I can't believe that I needed to explain my alibi to you."

He touched her hand lightly and said, "I never doubted you but like to have the facts." He added, "Was there a hint in your mother's video?"

"No such luck," she replied.

CHAPTER 34

Ava's funeral, held on July 20, was the third in a row in less than a month's time that the family had to plan and attend. Unlike Norma and Zabel's service, where a minimum of mourners attended, Ava's interment drew a small crowd. Not only did she have lots of friends, but the circumstances of her premature death attracted a curious bunch of people.

During the ritual in the cemetery one of Ava's acquaintances whispered to a friend, "Look over there, that was her newest husband."

"He seems nice," commented the other.

"Oh, and there's Emma, Ava's daughter. She looks overwhelmed, poor girl. Can you imagine, first she loses her grandmother and less than a month later, her mother gets murdered."

Similar sentiments were harbored among the mourners but most stayed in people's minds only, not spoken out loud.

There was a catered reception at the house serving appetizers and drinks, and with most of the furniture gone, the family had to rent folding tables and chairs for the occasion.

Derek was regretting the family's decision to have the reception as soon as it was under way. In his opinion the questions he was bombarded with were not only rude but hard to deal with, let alone to answer. On the other hand, being among strangers was a welcomed distraction.

Ever since Ava's strangulation, Derek could no longer cling to his belief that Zabel's murder had been committed by a stranger. The two killings obviously were connected, and Ava's appeared to have been a direct consequence of her lecturing the family the day before she went on her last jog.

The attitude between members of the entire household had become intolerable. They tried to stay out of each other's way whenever possible. And yes, everyone was on alert and watched their own backs. He wished that he and Margo could leave, but Lieutenant Krop had made it clear that they all had to stay in town.

He couldn't believe his ears when Stella made her selfish remark by saying, "I hope Lieutenant Krop knows what he's doing and wraps the case up in a hurry, or we have to cancel our river cruise." How selfish can you get? he thought. We just lost our sister.

The sale of the house was no longer Derek's top priority. His sole wish was that the mess they found themselves in would come to an end.

CHAPTER 35

After the funeral, the Uber driver dropped Emma off at her Airbnb, where she plopped onto the bed and finally was able to let herself go. Her sobbing exploded in loud, uncontrolled spurts.

Her life had become a nightmare ever since the phone call Julius made to her in Florence, Italy. She had been trying to concentrate on her studies and not dwell on the loss of her dear grandma, when he had hit her with the shocking news. She would never forget his words nor her own:

"I am sorry to have to tell you that your mom died and that you'll have to cut your foreign exchange program short and come home."

"What? Never mind my program. Tell me I didn't hear correctly."

"I know this comes as a shock but it's true. Your mother is dead."

"An accident?"

"No. She was strangled while on her morning jog."

"Oh my God! Is there a serial killer loose in Laguna Beach?"

"There is an ongoing inside investigation."

"What does that mean?"

"The culprit seems to be one of the family."

The horrible fact that Mom had been murdered was hard enough to deal with. But that one of her relatives could be responsible was beyond acceptance.

She calmed down as her weeping became silent, with a steady stream of tears rolling down her face. After the shocking news, she had packed her suitcase, said good-bye to classmates and teachers, and boarded the next available flight back to Los Angeles.

On the 12-hour flight home, she had tried to sleep, then watched a movie, but it was useless. She could not concentrate on anything but her sad situation. She had barely gotten settled in Florence when Mom had called, letting her know that Grandma had passed away. She had known in advance that it was coming, but the news still hit her hard.

She and Grandma had been close as far back as she could remember. While the steady humming sound of the plane almost felt comforting, she remembered Grandma's words before she started college on the East Coast, "If I die while you're away, don't come to my funeral. I want you to remember me alive and well."

Emma pondered how she had looked out the window of the plane, whispering to the clouds, "Yes, Grandma, I will always remember you full of life."

That phone call from Mom was the last she had heard from her and now she was also gone. Her Uncle Derek had suggested that she stay at Grandma's house with everyone else, but she could not do it. Julius's words, *the culprit seems to be one of the family,* were impossible to get out of her mind.

I can't trust my aunts and uncles, she thought, and I hardly know Julius, my stepfather. Stepfather? she mused. I can't bring myself to look at him as a father figure. I met the man once before arriving here, at Mom's wedding. Her wedding! She was so happy then, and now she's dead.

Everything that happened since her arrival in Laguna Beach felt like a bad dream she was going to wake up from at any moment. She did not know if jet lag was to blame for her sleepless nights or if they were the cause of grief. And today's funeral, especially the reception, had been the pits. All those people, mostly strangers to her, had said stupid things like, "Sorry for your loss," or "My deepest sympathy," and the worst of all, "I feel for you." They had no idea what it felt like to have your mother murdered.

CHAPTER 36

Lieutenant Krop sat idle at his desk, mulling over Ava's and Zabel's homicides. Was there really any merit in what Ava's husband had told him about the two Lutzer paintings? Julius Vazquez may have made the entire thing up in order to implicate one of the immediate family as the criminal.

But then, he reflected, Ava did make certain claims about those paintings and apparently did some finger pointing at her siblings the day before she was strangled. He not only learned this from Julius, but Derek also acknowledged the fact during his interrogation.

The story that the late Norma Davenport would have her heirs go on a scavenger hunt for some missing portraits worth a small fortune was hard to swallow. On the other hand, the lady appeared to have been an eccentric.

Ava may have made other accusations when giving her so-called speech that I know nothing about, considered the detective. Her husband may have only told me part of her discussion. Having everyone else sitting through another interrogation would be useless. They may secretly suspect one another, but they were in essence a tightknit family.

He gave up. I'll figure it out in the end, he told himself, and concentrated on paperwork of other cases that had been piling up on his desk. One of those cases, a burglary, took him to the other end of town.

When driving by the Brunt Gallery, he decided to have a quick chat with Sebastian.

He found him in his office and asked, "Mr. Brunt, do you have a minute? This won't take long."

Sebastian carefully sat down the artifact he had been holding and said, "Sure. This must be about Ava's tragedy. I'm sorry for that family, so what can I do to help?"

"That's right. I understand that you are friends with the Davenports," said the lieutenant.

"Not with the entire family. My wife and I hang out with Elliot and Paulette, on occasion."

"Since you not only own and manage this gallery but are also an art collector, I'm seeking your expert opinion."

"Yes?"

"Where would one keep a couple of valuable paintings if one chose not to display them on a wall?"

Sebastian grinned and said, "You are talking about the portraits *Betrothed I and Betrothed II* by Franz Lutzer."

Surprised, the lieutenant asked, "So your friends confided in you?"

"They sure did, while we enjoyed dinner at my house. Elliot told us all about Ava's lashing out at the family that same day. Not all of it was news to me, though. I already knew about the Lutzer paintings. It so happened that Ava herself had called me earlier that day, wanting to know the approximate worth of the portraits."

"I'll be darned. It's a small world!"

"To your question, paintings in their frames are practically impossible to conceal. It would take great resourcefulness in order to hide them."

"I'll be darned," repeated the detective.

Sebastian added, "I gave the story Ava told some thought. Elliot said that they had left no stone unturned in that house, looking for the paintings, so they were obviously not to be found at the Davenport residence. At first, I assumed that Ava made the entire thing up. My reasoning was that she had been influenced by seeing the two portraits at the live production of the *Pageant of the Masters* and had let her imagination run wild.

"But later I changed my mind. There had to be a good reason why she wanted to know the paintings' value. It couldn't just have been curiosity, like she wanted me to believe."

He smiled and stated, "My guess is that Mrs. Norma Davenport either sold the artwork or gave it to someone for safekeeping. And if the latter, I wouldn't be surprised if Zabel knew who that person was."

Lieutenant Krop got up to leave and said, "You've given me lots of food for thought. Thank you!"

CHAPTER 37

The day after the funeral Emma became restless. She needed answers to her unspoken questions. Her grief had turned into anger and she needed to vent it. Not paying attention where she was going, she marched out of her Airbnb and after a mile's walk stood at the hotel entrance where Uncle Derek and Aunt Margo lodged.

She hesitated for a second, then entered the lobby where the concierge called her relatives' room and then said, "Mrs. Davenport is in and said to send you right up to her suite."

Greeting Emma at the door, her aunt said, "What a nice surprise! Come on in."

Emma walked past her and waited until the door closed behind them, then burst out, "This is not a friendly visit. I'm done with everyone keeping secrets. I have a right to know what was going on with Mom before she was killed. When Julius drove me here from the airport, I tried to get information out of him, but he said that it was a family matter and I should ask my aunts and uncles. Then, when I tried to do that, everyone was busy making funeral arrangements."

Margo said, "Please calm down and have a seat."

After they were seated on upholstered chairs in the entry of the suite, Margo said, "There wasn't an occasion to have that chat, since you chose not to stay either at the house or at the hotel with us. Your Uncle Derek is vexed about that, by the way."

"You can hardly blame me for not getting cozy with my mom's murderer."

Margo bit her lip. That comment hurt, but she tried not to show it.

"Okay," she said, "I'll tell you what I know, which isn't much, but here goes." And she related the facts as she knew them, starting with the video Emma's grandmother had left behind; Zabel's accident, which had turned out to be no accident but homicide; and ending with the accusation her mother had confronted the family with on the day before she died.

Emma heard her out and then said, "I can't believe that one of you would kill twice for the sake of two lousy paintings."

"I have a hard time coping with it too."

"What kind of paintings is all that fuss about anyhow?"

Margo stated, "I never saw them, but according to your mom, they were oil paintings. To be specific, two separate portraits of a young engaged couple, created by the 19th Century painter Franz Lutzer."

Emma was no art connoisseur, but she had heard of Lutzer and guessed that paintings by him were not running cheap. She also had known Grandma well enough to picture her having fun with making up a game of hide and seek for her heirs.

There was a long pause before she asked, "What did the police find out?"

"There is an ongoing investigation but no arrest so far. A Lieutenant Krop is in charge and I sure hope he solves the case soon. We are all on edge, as you can imagine."

Up until that moment, Emma had not considered looking at the tragedy from her relatives' points of view. The ones that are innocent are suffering too, she now thought.

As she was ready to leave, Margo said, "We didn't get a chance to tell you, but your grandma mentioned you specifically in her will. You inherit her ruby jewelry."

"You mean the stunning ruby-and-diamond ring?"

"The entire set: a chain neckless with a ruby pendant, the ring you just described, and the matching earrings."

Touched, Emma remarked, "So Grandma remembered that rubies are my favorites."

***

Later in the day when Emma was back in her Airbnb mulling over the talk she'd had with Aunt Margo, she vaguely remembered text messages with a couple of photo attachments Grandma had sent more than half a year ago. The texts had not made sense to her and she had been busy studying for finals at the time. She had planned to have another look at them and the pictures later but realized now that she must have forgotten all about it.

Emma never deleted any texts, so she scrolled, trying to find those old ones from Grandma. The two had texted each other numerous times in the six months since, but she found the ones in question.

There were two photos and written comments with each. The first was of two paintings side by side, portraying a young woman and a young man. They were old-fashioned paintings and since Emma was not savvy in art, she did not know they were by Franz Lutzer. The corresponding text read, "*Now you see them.*" The next photo was of two landscape paintings, also side by side, and its text read, "*Now you don't.*"

Grandma had sent the following third text, "*Since you are my favorite grandchild, I'm giving you a hint.*" In answer Emma had sent her own text, informing Grandma that she was clueless what the pictures and the writing meant. To which she got the reply, "*You'll figure it out when the time comes. You are a smart cookie.*"

Emma stared at the photos and text messages and realized that the portraits she was looking at must be the missing paintings Margo had talked about, and the landscape pictures must be Zabel's work. But what does it all mean? she asked herself. *Now you see them. Now you don't.* What does it all mean?

She puzzled over it for a long time, until her head hurt but could not make sense of it. "Dear Grandma," she cried out aloud, "maybe I'm not the smart cookie you believed me to be, after all."

CHAPTER 38

The Davenport clan did not take the order "Don't leave town" literally. Each one had left the area on several occasions, figuring that as long as they returned to the house and slept in Laguna Beach each night, they were blameless.

Derek had left to attend business meetings in person in order to show his employees that their boss was not only instructing them remotely but kept on top of things. Elliot had driven away to work out at the gym of his own hometown more than once. Stella had gone shopping at the largest mall in Orange County, and she also spent most of one day playing Bunco at a friend's house in her neck of the woods.

As far as the in-laws, Margo had met in person with authors she was currently editing manuscripts for. Paulette had attended a wedding shower several towns away, and Lucas had spent a day as spectator at a Motocross. Julius was a gambler and had snuck away to visit Indian casinos on a couple of occasions. They all seemed to have taken steps to keep their sanity, was one way of looking at it.

Lieutenant Krop was aware of their escapades out of his domain. Officers in their unmarked cars, including his own, had taken turns keeping an eye out for the Davenport residence. As long as they all still lodged there, he had not been worried.

Only since he had learned about the missing paintings did the knowledge that each had driven out of the area become a concern. The artwork in question could have left town long ago, he now realized.

There was no point in worrying about spilled beans. When the time was right, he would get a court order for a search warrant. Until then, he kept busy building the case and gathering evidence. At least he was now confident he knew the motive for Zabel and Ava's homicides.

CHAPTER 39

On Saturday afternoon, July 22, Lilly landed at the Los Angeles airport. By the time she arrived home, it was already evening L.A. time. She was too tired to figure out what time it was in Sydney, New South Wales, nor whether it was day or night there.

Her three-week trip to Australia had been full of adventures but she was glad to be home. The light on her landline answering machine was flashing rapidly, and she was sure the thing was loaded with messages, but she didn't have the stamina to listen to them. It could wait another day. Any important calls would come via her cellphone.

With all the pressing chores awaiting her after a long absence - - like sorting through the mail a neighbor had kindly collected for her, food shopping, and doing laundry - - she did not get around to checking the answering machine until Sunday evening.

She listened to a slew of messages, most of them unimportant telemarketing calls. She suddenly paid attention when she heard two messages from the Davenports. On the first one, the person just said that it was about Zabel and to please call them. The second was to inform her that Zabel had passed away.

There were also two messages from a Lieutenant Krop of the Laguna Beach City Police Department, but Lilly hardly took in what he said. All she could think of was, *Zabel is dead. I can't believe it.*

She called the number provided. Stella answered, and the conversation went like this:

Lilly said, "I came home from a trip to Australia and got your messages about Zabel. Tell me I heard wrong and she isn't dead."

"I'm afraid it's true," answered Stella.

"She seemed in perfect health when she stayed with me."

Stella could not bring herself to tell Zabel's friend the full facts and only said, "She drove her Tesla into a building and died of internal injuries."

"That's awful!"

"I'm so sorry you were out of town and couldn't attend her service."

Lilly, not a fan of funerals, said, "I'd rather remember her alive and well."

After they ended the call, she thought, Zabel was so excited to have inherited the Tesla. Too bad she could only enjoy driving it for a short time. Then she reminisced about her friend's visit on that weekend, less than a month ago. Of how she had convinced Zabel to move to the Pasadena area, where she would have better job opportunities and a greater choice of finding the right home for her. The big bonus would be that they'd see one another more often.

Her thoughts drifted to the secret Zabel had kept concerning her employer, the late Norma Davenport. She remembered the advice she had given her friend by saying, "Now is the time to let the family know about it." Whether she had taken her up on it was something she would never know. She could have asked the lady she'd talked to on the phone but didn't think of it at that moment, too overcome by the bad news.

Lilly listened to the messages of the police officer again. The first one only gave his name, Lieutenant Krop, and a number to call. The second message he left was, "I have urgent information about Zabel Azarian. Please call at your earliest convenience."

Of course, she told herself. The police needed someone to identify Zabel after the accident. But how did this lieutenant obtain her phone number? The Davenports must have identified her, she reflected, and weeks later, the information the police wanted was hardly urgent any longer. Oh, but what he said was that *he* had urgent information for *me*.

It must be that he was going to let me know about Zabel's fatal accident, she mused. Out of courtesy, I'll call Lieutenant Krop on Monday, letting him know that I'm already aware of the sad news.

CHAPTER 40

Lieutenant Krop spent his Sunday with his wife and two boys at the Alta Laguna Park, known as the hilltop park because of its great view to the pacific ocean. There were many amenities to choose from at this huge recreation park: a playground, a soccer field, tennis courts, a half basketball court, and the newest craze, pickleball courts.

While his wife was reserving a table at the picnic area, the lieutenant played pickleball with his grade-school-age boys. They did not keep score but hit the balls back and forth, with the boys on one side of the net against their dad on the other. The kids did well, making Dad run for the ball on many of their shots.

With temperatures in the eighties on that cloudless day, they soon worked up a sweat and the lieutenant said, "Time out for lunch."

Their picnic of sandwiches, peanut butter and jelly for the boys and turkey avocado for mom and dad, tasted better up there on top of the world than at home. There was plenty of bottled water to keep everyone well hydrated. The lieutenant, dressed in shorts and a t-shirt, may have looked off-duty, but his mind could never fully relax when on a mind-boggling case.

Two ladies walked by their table, deep in conversation. He overheard one say, "It's not about the money - - -"

That fragment of their discussion stuck with the lieutenant for the rest of the day. The unfinished sentence stayed with him later in the afternoon, when all four of them rode their bicycles on the park's trails, and would not leave him alone after turning in at night.

It's not about the money! He lay in bed, looking at the two homicides from a different perspective. His photographic memory kicked in as he visualized in his mind's eye two separate interviews he had had with one person and the observations he had made at that time. Yes, it all fit! Now, proving it was a different matter.

His wife was also still awake and said, "The boys had a great day today, and so did we. Let's finishing it by making it perfect."

"A good idea!" he said, as he reached for her.

And so the lieutenant could put his case out of mind, at long last.

CHAPTER 41

The puzzle about those texts from Grandma did not leave Emma any peace. She had mulled over it numerous times, without success. On Monday morning, while scrutinizing the pictures and their accompanying text once more, she finally had a brainstorm. She was thinking out of the box now and may be wrong, but it would be typical of Grandma to scheme it all and make a game out of it.

An hour later, she showed up at Margo's hotel suite doorstep once again.

The editor was making corrections to a complicated paragraph of her current work and said, "Sorry, Emma, I'm on a deadline and don't have time to talk today."

"This won't take long."

"Come on in then and have a seat," Margo said, and went back to her laptop to press 'Save' in order not to lose her place.

When they faced one another, Emma said, "Tell me exactly why Zabel went to the auction house the day she returned from visiting her friend."

"I already told you. She went to retrieve her five paintings."

"Yes, that's what you said, but did she actually get her artwork back?" Emma wanted to know.

"She did."

"Where is it now?"

Margo replied, "The officer in charge brought all her pastels back with her other possessions. But I don't think you should dwell on those things. It's not good for you."

"I'm a big girl. So where are Zabel's works now?"

"I believe they are at the house in what used to be Zabel's room. None of us wanted them. They're too much of a reminder of what happened."

Emma stated, "We can't ignore what happened and need to get at the truth."

"Please don't try to play detective. That's what got your mom into trouble." Margo bit her lip as soon as those words escaped her. "I'm so sorry!" she added.

"That's okay. And don't worry, I'm not going to play at anything. What's the officer's name again, the one in charge of the investigation?"

"Lieutenant Krop of the Laguna Beach City Police Department."

After the young woman left, Margo was not sure whether to be relieved or worried.

CHAPTER 42

By that Monday morning, the lieutenant's conclusion had turned into a certainty, as he mulled over the events, step by step since Zabel's homicide. Everything made sense and he was sure to have arrived at the truth. He had motive and opportunity for the two crimes, but what about proof? All evidence he could come up with was circumstantial. There was no DNA, no fingerprints, no weapon.

Was he ready to confront the killer? Could he get a search warrant with the facts he had gathered so far? The answer was 'no' to both questions.

He buried his face into both hands in frustration as the phone rang:

"Hello, Lieutenant Krop here."

"Hello, Lieutenant. I came back from a trip and found your two messages on my landline about my friend Zabel."

"Is your name Lilly?"

"Yes. I want to let you know that I already heard the sad news about Zabel's accident."

"It wasn't an accident. Zabel Azarian was murdered."

There was a gasp. Then silence. The lieutenant was not sure whether she was still on the line.

Then she said, "That's horrific." After another pause, she stated, "But I was told that she drove her car into a building."

"Correct. But she was drugged first," said the lieutenant. "I originally called you in the hopes that you could shed some light on the case."

"Me?"

"From the Davenports I learned that Zabel had spent the weekend before she died at your residence, and that the two of you were good friends. She may have taken you into her confidence about what was going on in her life."

Lilly replied, "She had just lost her employer, who was also her friend, but you must already know that. Anyhow, she was thinking of relocating to my general area."

"Apart from that, did she share anything else?"

Lilly debated with herself whether to tell the lieutenant what her friend had disclosed. In the end, she didn't think it would make a difference to Zabel at this point.

So she said, "She had something else on her mind but it can't possibly have anything to do with her death. She was keeping a secret of Norma Davenport's and I told her that since her employer had passed away, she was no longer bound by her promise."

"I agree. And that secret may be crucial to my investigation."

"I doubt that. It was about a couple of paintings."

Lieutenant Krop almost jumped out of his office seat and stated, "Don't say another word about this over the phone. I know that you live in Arcadia, and Laguna Beach is too far out of your way to give me a statement in person. May I send an officer over to your house to take down your formal statement?"

"No problem, but it will have to be today or tomorrow. Starting on Wednesday, I'm back at work and will only be home evenings."

"I can arrange for somebody to be at your residence this afternoon."

He asked for her address before they ended the call.

Lilly walked away from her landline in a haze. The news of Zabel's fatal accident had been bad enough, but now that she knew that her friend was murdered, she had an even worse time coping with the idea. The police officer had not given her much information, only that Zabel had been drugged before crashing her car. Naturally, he would not tell her who the suspects were. That would be against police policy, she was sure.

Still jet-lagged, she was glad to have two extra days before returning to work, teaching the summer semester at Pasadena City College. Oh, but I can't be a lady of leisure; somebody will show up this afternoon to take my statement. I'd better hop in the shower right now.

CHAPTER 43

After Lilly's phone call, the lieutenant was full of excitement. He finally had the break he was waiting for. When he had made that call to Lilly three weeks ago, he knew that it was a long shot, but now it had paid off. According to Lilly, the secret Zabel had kept was about a couple of paintings. It sure sounded to him that she had information about the hiding place of those two Lutzer portraits.

He lost no time and arranged for an officer of the court to take down Lilly's statement. If he was lucky, the document would be faxed to him within 24 hours.

The detective was on a roll. On that Monday afternoon, he received another unexpected call, this time from Ava Vazquez's daughter, Emma.

The young woman said, "I'm almost sure I know what my grandma did with the Lutzer paintings."

"Interesting," said the lieutenant, not knowing if he could take her seriously.

"I figured it out by studying some photos she sent me in a couple of text messages."

"Wait a minute. You're talking about your grandmother, Norma Davenport?"

"Yes."

"I'm sorry, but the lady has passed away."

"The text messages are from half a year ago. At that time I was totally clueless. The pictures and Grandma's comment about them made no sense to me until today, when I finally figured the thing out."

Lieutenant Krop's radar was on alert now, and he said, "I'd like to see you in person as soon as possible."

To which Emma replied, "That's what I was going to suggest. I need to show you my phone so you can see for yourself what I'm talking about. I don't have a car but can call an Uber to take me to your police station."

"No need. I can swing by to pick you up. Are you staying at the Davenport residence?"

"No, I'm at an Airbnb in town."

"In that case, I have a better idea. I'll come see you," he said.

CHAPTER 44

This time the lieutenant parked at the back parking lot of the Brunt Gallery, walked up to the delivery entrance, and peeked into the window adjacent to it. When he saw Sebastian sitting at his desk, he tapped the window lightly.

The former was on the phone and motioned to the lieutenant to wait, thinking, what does the man want now?

After hanging up, Sebastian went to open the back door and joked, "You must be on a secret mission, sneaking in the back. Can it wait, though? I'm extremely busy today."

"No, sir, I'm afraid it can't."

Sebastian led the way to his office and said, "Have a seat. What's on your mind?"

The lieutenant stated, "I'm about to make an arrest."

"That's great news! So you don't need my help after all. Who's the criminal?"

"Stop the charade, Mr. Brunt. I figured it out. You were clever, but not clever enough."

"You can't possibly think that I'm the culprit."

"I don't think so. I know so."

Sebastian got up from behind his desk and walked a few paces back and forth in the small office, like a caged animal. Whether to calm his nerves or give himself time to think what to say next was unclear.

He sat back down and appeared calm as he said, "Your accusation is unfounded, but I'm going to humor you and listen to how you arrived at your allegation."

The lieutenant did just that. He started by explaining, "I have a photographic memory and can recall conversations and/or observations word for word. Naturally, at the end of the day, I'll write a report, but during my investigation, I can revisit accurately what I've learned from interviewing suspects.

"On the surface you smelled like a rose. When I came to see you that first time at your auction house, I was mainly concerned about Zabel's movements right after she left your premises. At that time I thought that her killer had followed her or had a pre-arranged rendezvous with the woman. You and I both know that this was not the case.

"You made two mistakes during that first interview, even though I was not aware of them until much later in my investigation. The first was telling me that you took two of Zabel's paintings out of their frames. When I asked you why, you explained it away by saying that those frames were valuable and that you would sell them separately. That made sense to me at the time, but now I know better.

"Your second error was that you drew attention to the fact that Zabel's accident happened around the corner of your office. That statement of yours helped me later, since I knew that the sleeping pills took only minutes to take effect."

Sebastian opened his mouth but before he could utter a word, the lieutenant held up a hand and continued, "At first glance, your alibi for the crucial time implicated in Zabel's killing looked foolproof. It was a fact that you spent the entire time at your gallery. At that point I was also not aware that you had a motive. In fact, before I heard of the missing paintings, none of my suspects seemed to have a motive for the crimes.

"During our first talk in your office at the Brunt Gallery, you gave me information about a car you noticed parked on the street, overlooking the parking lot of your auction house. You told me the truth: There was a white Mercedes with someone in the driver seat parked when you helped Zabel load her paintings into the Tesla.

"I now realize that you milked that info for all it was worth in order to draw attention away from yourself. It worked. For a while, I suspected the driver of that Mercedes as the villain. At that same visit I noticed the convenience of the Brunt Gallery's back parking lot.

"It was not until my second visit to your office here that you made the biggest blunder. I asked, 'Where would one keep a couple of paintings if one chose not to display them?' You replied, 'Paintings in their frames are practically impossible to conceal.' On that day I was ignorant of the significance of your statement; it only rang a bell recently. I had come to you to seek advice from an expert and did not consider you a suspect at that point."

Sebastian kept a nonchalant attitude and said, "This is all extremely entertaining and well-imagined, but far from the truth."

Ignoring the interruption, the lieutenant continued, "As for Ava's strangulation, when I suspected one of the family as the culprit, I strolled and drove around the neighborhood, timing a walk or drive from the Davenport residence to the scene of the crime. But it was not until the last couple of days that I made it my business to locate your private residence. Your house is also in the immediate neighborhood where Ava's body was found."

He looked out the window and remarked, "Your delivery entrance here came in handy to let Zabel into your office unnoticed." He glanced around the room and pointed to a small refrigerator, saying, "I bet you there was lemonade in that fridge on the day Zabel was killed. Is there lemonade there now?"

Not getting an answer, the lieutenant added, "The forensics team discovered a fresh lemonade stain on Zabel's blouse. It must have been easy for you to add several sleeping pills to her lemonade before handing it to her."

There was a dangerous flicker in Sebastian's eye, but he did not lose his cool and said, "You made a bunch of accusations - - I take that back, they're more like suggestions - - but you can't prove any of it. Most of all, I had no motive to kill Zabel or Ava."

"That's where you are wrong. I stumbled on the motive last Sunday while on a picnic in the park. I overheard a fragment of conversation, 'It's not about the money.' I had assumed that the guilty person was after the cash those Lutzer paintings would fetch, but that bit of dialogue made it all clear to me. It's not about the money; it's about a fanatic art amasser who *had to have* the famous *Betrothed I and Betrothed II* portraits in his private art collection.

"The motive in Ava's case was self-preservation. You knew or guessed that she suspected one of her family to have committed the crime, but could not take the chance that eventually she would put two and two together and learn the truth."

The lieutenant went on, "As for proof, I have two witnesses that will give evidence in a court of law."

An anger vein appeared on Sebastian's forehead as he raised his voice, asking, "What witnesses?"

"One was a friend of Zabel's who knows the secret about the paintings. I am in possession of her statement, which is explanatory. The other is a young woman who figured it out and showed me how."

"That's all circumstantial," Sebastian protested.

"I am also in possession of search warrants for your gallery, your auction house, and most important, your private residence."

Sebastian knew it was over. He had been aware of the fact the minute Lieutenant Krop had set foot in his office with that determined look on his face. He had played along, not wanting to give up, but knew he was beat. The idea of police officers searching through his precious things, particularly in his house where he kept his cherished collection, gave him the shivers.

He announced, "There's no need to search my properties. I'm willing to confess."

"In that case," said the lieutenant, "Sebastian Brunt, I'm placing you under arrest for the murders of Zabel Azarian and Ava Vazquez," and he read him the Miranda rights while snapping the handcuffs around his wrists. Then he walked him out the back door.

CHAPTER 45

At the Laguna Beach City Police Department, Sebastian Brunt's confession was underway in the interrogation room. Lieutenant Krop was presiding, but other officers were also present. Everything was done by the book. Sebastian confessed to both murders. His confession did not ring true as a humble admission of guilt, but sounded more like cocky bragging of his cleverness. However, it was valid, recorded, taken down in writing, and then signed by him.

The following is Sebastian Brunt's confession of the homicide of Zabel Azarian:

"First and foremost, I want to make something clear. I am an avid art collector and adding valuable artwork into my private collection is my passion. I first thought that it was strange that two of Zabel's pastels were in such old-fashioned frames. The other three, by the way, sat in simple, contemporary frames. Already at first glance, when I saw Zabel's pastels hanging in the Davenport's living room, I had decided to sell those frames separately.

"At my auction house, as I took Zabel's two paintings out of their ornate frames and discovered Betrothed I and Betrothed

II by Franz Lutzer behind hers, separated only by a thin sheet of paper, I was ecstatic. I realized that the Davenport family had no idea of the rare find's existence, or its worth. At the time I did not know that Z. A. stands for Zabel Azarian and accepted all her pastels to be auctioned off.

"I have to hand it to old Mrs. Davenport. The whole idea, and executing it to perfection, was clever of her. I'm sure her companion helped with the work involved. Who would have thought they'd hide the Lutzer paintings behind Zabel's pastels? The lady must have had no idea that the works would leave her house, assuming her heirs would keep them. If I had not removed the frames, I would have been none the wiser myself.

"It is hard to describe the feeling I experienced when stumbling on the exquisite find. My heart was pounding, my ears were ringing, and my hands turned clammy. Then I pulled myself together and went to work with what needed to be done. There was no way I could keep the splendid portraits in plain view, not even at the house in my private art collection. At least not for a year or two, until the dust would settle, I told myself.

"So I took the canvases off their stretchers and rolled them up, in order that they would be easier to conceal. Naturally, even in that condition they could not withstand a thorough search. I also kept the frames and planned to eventually return the paintings to them. In time, I would be able to display the works in their proper place: my private collection.

"When Zabel stormed into my auction house, demanding to get her paintings back, I told her that I had already taken two of them out of their antique frames. 'Give me a day or so, and I'll put your pastels back into them,' I assured her. She wasn't worried about the frames she said, and that I should not play games with her. She wanted all the artwork back, hers plus the two Franz Lutzer oil paintings.

"I had to come up with a plan quickly and told her that the two masterpieces were not in my possession at that moment, because they were being authenticated by an expert. I stated that I was planning to meet the art expert at my gallery in the early afternoon, and that she should join us.

"'Park in the back lot and I'll let you in at the rear door in about 15 minutes from now,' I told her. I assured Zabel that when we got the result, regardless of whether the paintings were genuine or only copies, I would give them back to the family.

"All nonsense. I am an authority on fine arts and could easily perform the necessary tests. I knew that the two Lutzer were originals and had no plans of giving them back. How could I? A find of a lifetime had fallen into my lap and in time would have a place of honor in my private collection. The good trusting soul that Zabel was, she believed my story. I even buttered her up by telling her that I thought her five pastels were great.

"I made sure that I had a witness when Zabel left the rear parking lot of my auction house and asked an employee to help carry her five paintings and load them into her Tesla. I needed to establish that I was still there when she drove off. And as luck had it, I saw a car parked on the street behind my lot with someone inside reading the paper.

"I thought that fact may come in handy at one point. Sure enough, I was able to point it out to the detective in charge, who deduced that the person in that car followed Zabel when she left my place.

"I also made sure to arrive at the front entrance of the gallery in plain view, greeting and talking to several people, as I made my way to my office at the rear. When the coast was clear, and I was sure there were no witnesses, I let Zabel in the back door.

"As we waited for the non-existing expert, I offered her a beverage - - it was a hot day in July - - where I could easily

add a slew of sleeping pills, without her being the wiser. Then I pretended to get a call from the expert and told her that the man needed to change the appointment for later in the day. 'Come back at 3 o'clock when he'll be here,' I said.

"I'm a poor sleeper, especially when traveling. Consequently, I always carry sleeping pills on my person, just in case. As one can see, that fact came in handy the day Zabel turned up at my turf.

"We know what happened next. She fell asleep at the wheel and crashed her car. Of course, I couldn't be sure that she'd die but was certain that she'd at least end up in the hospital with critical injuries, and if necessary, I was prepared to finish the job there."

The following is Sebastian Brunt's confession of the homicide of Ava Vazquez:

"I strangled Ava in self-protection, so to speak. When she called, I was sure she was either on to me or soon would be. I knew she was jogging by our house early every morning, so I formed the plan to eliminate her.

"By coincidence or providence, however one looks at it, on the evening after her call, Carla and I had Elliot and Paulette over for dinner. To my surprise, I learned that Ava suspected one of the family was Zabel's killer. Before going to bed that night, I had second thoughts about eliminating Ava. She did not seem to suspect me, at least not yet. But I could not take the chance that eventually she would not discover the truth. So I went ahead with my plan the very next morning.

"Getting rid of Ava and walking back to my house only took six minutes. I timed myself. Then I hopped back into bed where my wife was still asleep. I knew that she would think that I had never left and would swear to it."

EPILOGUE

Sebastian spent the rest of his life in prison. In order to spare his wife from additional humiliation of a house search, he revealed the exact location of the two rolled up portraits to the authorities. The Davenport family engaged an expert who returned them to their stretchers. The original frames were also found, allowing *Betrothed I and Betrothed II* to resume their proper places.

The two paintings were sold to an art museum and the proceeds divided by the remaining three siblings and Emma, who inherited her mother's share, since Julius was bound by the prenuptial agreement. Thanks to the recent provenance added to those portraits by Franz Lutzer, they fetched more than their thief had estimated.

The family decided to offer Zabel's five pastels to her friend Lilly, who accepted them with enthusiasm. She loved the landscape scenes, but that was not the only reason she cherished them. Hanging in her condominium, they would be a reminder of her dear friend and at the same time carried with them a bit of dramatic history.

Sebastian's arrest and therefore the last chapter of the case, as far as Lieutenant Krop was concerned, took place on July 25 - - in time for Stella and Lucas to board their river cruise, after all.

As to the fate of Norma Davenport's home in Laguna Beach, the family decided not to sell the house. The property would be rented to students from fall to early spring - - the University of California, Irvine, being a short drive away - - at an affordable rate. During the tourist season in late spring and summer, the rent would be doubled. And most important, family members had top priority to use their property as a vacation home during those months of high demand, if they chose.

In regards to the morale of the Davenport clan, it would be a while before they could forgive one another. Even if understandable under the circumstances, suspecting your own family members of murder is not easily forgotten.

The late Norma Davenport had not had an inkling of what her bit of mischievous fun would trigger.

Elliot summed it up by stating, "Mom's joke turned lethal in the end."

A Note from the Author

Just like all characters in this book of fiction are not real people, I also took the liberty of inventing an artist and his work of art. Franz Lutzer did not exist in the 19th Century, nor did his paintings, titled *Betrothed I and Betrothed II*. On the other hand, the *Pageant of the Masters* in Laguna Beach does exist and its production has been held in the summer months for decades. It is also a fact that Leonardo Da Vinci's *The Last Supper* is portrayed in the show most years.

Stand-Alone Mysteries by Alice Zogg

A Lethal Joke
A Dark Book Club
A Bad Apple
Exposing the Past
No Curtain Call
The Ill-Fated Scientist
Accidental Eyewitness
A Bet Turned Deadly

R. A. Huber Mysteries by Alice Zogg

Evil at Shore Haven
Guilty or Not
Murder at the Cubbyhole
Revamp Camp
Final Stop Albuquerque
The Fall of Optimum House
The Lonesome Autocrat
Tracking Backward
Turn the Joker Around
Reaching Checkmate